Dying of Thinking

THE FRENCH LIST

PASCAL QUIGNARD

Dying of Thinking

The Last Kingdom IX

TRANSLATED BY JOHN TAYLOR

LONDON NEW YORK CALCUTTA

**PAP
TAGORE**

www.bibliofrance.in

The work is published with the support of the
Publication Assistance Programmes of the Institut français

Seagull Books, 2023

Originally published as *Mourir de penser*
© Éditions Grasset & Fasquelle, 2014

First published in English by Seagull Books, 2023
English translation © John Taylor, 2023

ISBN   978 1 80309 242 3

British Library Cataloguing-in-Publication Data
A catalogue record for this book is available from the British Library

Typeset and designed by Seagull Books, Calcutta, India
Printed and bound by Hyam Enterprises, Calcutta, India

CONTENTS

In the year 699, the Frisians consented to convert to Christianity. In the month of March 700, on the first day of the year, the first and foremost among them, Redbad, King of the Frisians, standing before his assembled tribes, prepared himself to be baptized. He was already completely naked and had put one foot in the font when he suddenly had a doubt and, hesitating to sink his other foot into the holy water, worryingly asked the priest, who was getting ready to baptize him:

'But where are my ancestors?'

No response.

Whereupon the King of the Frisians lifted his eyes. He looked at the Christian priest. The priest remained motionless. He had begun to raise his hand. In order to kill off demons, he was readying to toss some salt around the man who was going to immerse himself.

The King reiterated his question:

'Where can the greatest number of my ancestors be found?'

The man of God, still silent, obstinately silent, kept his salt-filled hand raised in the air above the vat, waiting for the King of the Frisians to squat down completely inside it.

Full of wrath, Redbad raised his voice. For the third time he repeated his question and made it more specific. Where were his ancestors? Were his ancestors in hell? Could they be found in paradise?

The priest ended up turning his face towards Redbad.

He pronounced the word 'hell'.

When he learnt that all the kings who had preceded him and most of the members of his family were in hell, King Redbad removed the foot that he had slipped into the vat. He moved away from the priest, from the monks, from the baptismal pool. He went over to his knights, who were standing in the first row of the assembly. Speaking softly, he said to them:

'It is holier to follow the greatest number than the smallest number.'

And he left the church without turning back. Indeed, he was the only Frisian to act like this. Not only none of his subjects followed him, but none of his knights imitated his example. Even the companion who rode his horse alongside him in battles refused to accompany him. Three days went by. On the fourth day, King Redbad did not awake. He was found dead. His mouth had become black.

＊

'Sanctius est plures quam pauciores sequi.'

This is what King Rachordus said to the assembly of his knights. It is holier to follow the greatest number than the smallest number. This is democracy in action.

＊

In the *Golden Legend*, this little story follows, without any reason, the death of Bede the Venerable. The motivity of the scene is extraordinary. A hand is raised, showing a fistful of salt to the passing air; a foot is withheld, as if trying out the originary water that it does not reach. The Latin text force-fully expresses the suspense (King Redbad's suspended foot): Et jam unum pedem in lavacro, alterum retrahens . . . And already King Redbad had placed his foot in the font, withholding the other foot, withdrawing it, when he worryingly asked:

'Ubinam plures majorum suorum essent?'

In what place were his ancestors found?

Word for word: In what place were found the greatest number of his elders?

*

Belonging to a group is more pleasant than aloneness. Fecundity seems preferable to curiosity. Faithfulness to family history is more seductive than the eternal lucidity that comes from being in contact with God. Here, courage is needed to prefer the companionship of ancestors to eternal life. For we can rightfully think that he whom Voragine calls Rachordus sincerely believes in God. He makes a public speech to the assembly of his men-at-arms and his court. He truly renounces future immortality because of genealogical solidarity with his dead ancestors. Completely naked, shivering from the cold, holding one foot in his hand, his buttocks squatting on the edge of the polished granite vat, at the very instant when he is going to sink into the holy water, he suddenly and boldly thinks to himself: 'Better eternal hell with my dead ones than alone in paradise.' Tallemant des Réaux records this response by Malherbe:

'I lived like others. I want to die like others and go to the place where the others go.'

*

4

The calculation made by Rex Rachordus is statistical in nature. It implies a power struggle between two quantities of human beings. In his calculation, he compares the number of ancestors who have died and the number of living human beings around him. He asks the monk who is readying to frighten away the demons where the majority (plures) can be found. The translation could be made by skipping 'sequi': For the minority is less sacred than the majority. One can also call this point 'the monarchic error'. Rachordus, King of the Frisians, commits the same strategic error as Louis XVI, King of the French. The only thing that matters to him, beyond his realm, is the statistic that speaks for 'no singular individual' among each shouting person. Widespread acclamation, tumultuous crowd movements, public clamour, success, victory, the sales list, collective recognition, religious exaltation, recurrent media performances are all holy. The state of being an individual does not even represent a 'stage' in the evolution of societies and civilizations. Individual experience, otium, bold research, art, study, ecstasy, everything that removes one from one's family, everything that emancipates one from the group, everything that liberates one from spoken language, is damned.

Scholium 1. Faith is preferable to clear-sightedness. Happiness is preferable to curiosity.

Scholium 2. Oral communication and dialogues between classes or communities in conflict are preferable to the secret revolt of individuals and to the absolute silence shown by books.

*

The latter point no longer concerns the number but the nature of the mass of people used as a reference. What is the identity of the greatest mass? Who names 'plures'? The greatest mass is the mass that has constantly increased. What is the constantly increased mass? King Redbad is clear about this: he does not hesitate for a second about this point and this clarity is probably his main contribution to the legitimation beseeched by the effort of thinking. The crux of the process is sacrifice. The referent is the heap of the dead.

The 'heap of the dead' will always be the most important element in human societies because it increases by means of all the living human beings who join it in the memory of those who survive.

Scholium 3. The cumulative heap of the dead is the reference mass of human societies which use writing. From this stems the invention of tombs (stone cities of the beyond) at the dawn of Neolithic societies, that is, *prior to the cities of the living* which are left to woods, leaves, pieces of bark and animal hides.

*

Zwingli died while crying out:

'Your ancestors will also be there!'

The Catholics cut him up into pieces because they wanted to eat him as a wild beast. Myconius took his heart and threw it into the Rhine so that the Catholics would not tear it apart by devouring it, and make it their own while digesting it.

*

King Redbad looked down when he resolved to remove his foot from the water. He murmured while withdrawing his dripping toes and while lowering his eyelids: 'I prefer not to think, I prefer to belong.'

What is thinking? An inner *De bello civili*. An intestine civil war. Thought cannot accommodate itself to the exertion of a power that screens off one's curiosity. Pure *cur*. Wandering *Pourquoi*. Incessantly famished intellectual hunger (at least every five or six hours, thought again being on the alert during the day even as a penis is erect in the night, thought thirsting like an anguished throat, famished like a hollow stomach.)

Thought is no different from tentative thought, that is, from sexual voyeurism, from lack, from mental aporia, from social secession, from fright stimulating the brain, from a vital, animalistic gaze on any anomaly that puts the field in disorder.

A kind of questioning assuaged by no gaping response at the centre of psychic animation.

Scholium 4: anxious or desirous spying cannot be submitted to any mission or submission. The qui-vive—being on the alert—is vital.

*

The King of the Frisians stands on the edge of the vat like a heron on the edge of a pond.

Intinctum pedem retrahens . . .

But King Redbad, instead of dipping his other foot into the cold water, withdraws his right foot, which he had begun to sink into the water; he withdraws from the group surrounding him; he withdraws into himself, into his memory and, name by name, goes back up through all the dead in his lineage. He thinks: 'The socialization of the little ones who are born, who learn the language of their dead fathers on the lips of their living mothers, who join the group of elders, is more vital than the reflexion of subjects who grow old, who break away from and distrust all other human beings.'

Whereupon King Redbad withdraws to the back of the nave and thinks in the cold. This withdrawal into the shadows (this retraction into the back of the brain) means: 'However I envisage it, the act of thinking, in the depths of the psyche, will be less immortal than social reproduction.'

Jean Buridan's donkey—which inherits directly from the donkey of Apuleius of Madauros—hesitates in a similar way.

Dissociating oneself is the bucket of bran. Associating oneself is the bucket of oats.

Lucius the donkey chews the air above his buckets, not knowing how to choose between the bran and the oats.

In the stable, a kind of mist drifts up from his tormented lips and ends up effacing his eyes.

*

Thinking of the risk of losing the esteem of one's own, of the risk of leaving human odour, of the risk of moving away from the cemetery, of the risk of being banished from the city, of the risk of being excommunicated, of the risk of dying, killed by the French, in a solitary inn room. Such is Spinoza.

Morality is that which seeks to please the dead. Belief in any religion is immersed in the act of putting to death that was *acquired* when herbivorous troops *disguised* themselves as carnivorous packs and wanted to have the killed beast itself bless the blood that they had spilt when killing it. Such is Redbad.

Spinoza or Redbad.

Thinking or believing.

*

'Pauciores', Redbad says to his warriors to turn them away from God.

'The happy few', Stendhal said to his readers to turn them away from the national community.

One needs to understand Stendhal's use of English: There is *no word* in French to express a small number.

The Romans possessed the magic word 'paucitas'. This word should be imposed upon the French language. 'Paucité'—'paucity'—as opposed to majority.

*

Redbad is definite about this latter point: the Superego hates getting its feet wet.

Better having one's feet on dry land and the approbation of the others in the heat of hell than being in paradise alone.

He who thinks is thus in paradise. There is no doubt about this. However, in paradise, he is all alone, completely naked, without the dead, shivering, his two feet wet.

CHAPTER 2

One Can Die of Thinking I

Oistrakh and Stern were friends. They were genuine friends. This friendship lasted 20 years without ever failing. Only death, which accomplishes nothing, put an end to it. The last time that they saw each other, in London in 1974, Oistrakh was only 66 years old, but it seemed to Stern that he was completely exhausted. He had gained a lot of weight. (He would die three months later.) Isaac Stern took his friend's hand and said:

'You are tired, David.'

'Yes.'

'Leave your country. Come and take a rest.'

'I can't, Isaac. They won't let my wife and children travel with me.'

'So work less.'

'I can't. If I stop playing, I think. If I started thinking, I would die.'

CHAPTER 3

One Can Die of Thinking II

Ulysses in tatters is recognized by his old dog, Argos.

Two thousand and eight hundred years ago, Homer wrote in the *Odyssey* 17.301: *Enoesen Odyssea eggus eonta*. Word for word: He (the dog) *thought* 'Ulysses' in he who came up to him.

The scene is very moving because up to then no man or woman on the island of Ithaca had recognized Ulysses disguised as a beggar: it is his old dog, Argos, who suddenly recognizes the man. In European history, the first living being surprised while thinking is a dog.

It is a dog who *thinks* a man.

Let me come back to the scene. The dog is lying on the dung heap. The dog raises his head when he hears a voice near the door. He sees a beggar speaking with the swineherd. But the disguise doesn't fool the dog for long: he *thinks* Ulysses in the beggar.

Moreover, at the same moment, suddenly, it is Ulysses himself who *senses* that he is recognized in space (that someone 'is thinking' of him in the milieu, in the surroundings). Ulysses looks around. He at last spots his aged hunting dog, Argos, not far from the gate, lying on a pile of garbage and dirty straw, with whom 20 years before, when he was the king of the island, he would hunt boars, deer, hares, ibexes.

Ulysses by no means wants to be recognized. He hastily wipes away a tear running down his cheek dirtied beforehand with a piece of charred wood so that he would not be identifiable.

As to Argos, he lifts his eyes, sticks out his muzzle into the air, 'thinks' Ulysses inside the beggar, wags his tail, drops his two ears, dies.

He thinks and dies.

Therefore, the first being who thinks in Homer turns out to be a dog because the verb 'noein' (which is the Greek verb translated by 'to think') first meant 'to scent'. To think is to scent the new thing that surges forth in the surrounding air. It means to intimate beyond the tatters, beyond the face smeared black, within the false appearance, in the depths of the environment that keeps getting modified, the prey, a speed, time itself, a springing forth, a possible death. We come from a species for which predation dominated all contemplation. In Greek, the word for contemplation is theoria. The prey was swallowed up inside the devourer. The prey was not contemplable without an almost immediate aggression, without destruction following upon the vision and without its being thoroughly devoured down to the remains of its disjointed carrion by each satiated predator.

Once their own hunger was assuaged, only the scraps of the meal were contemplable: antlers, bones, teeth, fangs, tusks, furs, hides, carapaces, feathers, excrements, dung.

This is the first lexicon.

Anything standing out in the visual field, vestiges of the living, traces of the motivity of wild animals, mnemotechnies of their deaths, are as many letters (in Latin, litterae) forming the only contemplable thing.

Parmenides wrote that signs (in Greek, semata) are initially the excrements of beasts being pursued, then the tracks that indicate their trail, finally the stars (in Latin, sidera) that mark out their course.

Signs of passing beasts become the signs of recognition that guide hunters to their prey—until they are suddenly inverted and become the signs of the trail enabling them to return from the place of the quarry to the 'hearth', to the 'fire', to the 'coction' of dead, cut-up prey, to the possibility of a tale not only about hunting but also about survival

PASCAL QUIGNARD

among one's own while sitting in a circle around the flames
cooking the dead prey.

In Greek, a backwards movement is meta-phora.

In Chinese, the movement of turning back on a path
is tao.

The ancient Greeks of Turkey (like the ancient Chinese
of Taoism) thought of thinking as a going and returning:
noein and neomai. They think of thinking as a going that
does not forget the path on which it goes. A going that goes
all the while already returning: such is the path, the lane,
the way that makes up the depths of thought. Zhuang Zhou
writes: such is the tao. In the same period, Heraclitus writes
more skilfully: it is an enantiodromia (a course that retraces
its steps). This is why the first Greek thinkers, well before
philosophy takes shape, wished to found the word noos
(thought) in the word nostos (return). Thinking meant
wandering anywhere while, however, recalling how to be
able to come back alive among one's own after the ordeal
of death. There is a regret (in Latin, a regressus) even in the
boldness of thinking. There is a path that is not forgotten
in that which thinks. This is what the Greek word for
method (meta-hodos) means: the opposite direction (the
recapitulative way) in which, indeed, the trans-port (the
meta-phora) is carried out in reverse. There is something or
someone lost—*un perdu*—that incessantly loves itself in the

nostalgic movement of thinking. Are humans capable of thinking without a way back? No. One understands why Redbad first thinks, before making the decision to metamorphose his body, before sinking into the new originary water: 'Where have my dead ones gone?' A *regret* overcomes him and he flees the eternal water to find them, three days later, where most of them are: in the blackness of the other world where lie shrivelled up, under the ground, all the dead ones who come undone there.

This is how verse 326 of song 17 of Homer's *Odyssey* describes the strange *thanatos* (the voluptuousness, the deflation, the depression, the death) of the hunting dog in the instant immediately following his *noesis* (his sense of smell, his thought). The shadows of death cover Argos' eyes *just after* they have spotted Ulysses, whom they had been waiting to see for 20 years.

CHAPTER 4

Nagasena and King Menander

The *Milinda Panha* was drafted in Pali. It tells of the military expedition that the Greek king Menandros made in the upper Ganges region in ~122. He expands upon, embellishes, ameliorates a dialogue that actually took place between the monk Nagasena and King Milinda during the conquest of the Punjab. *Milinda* is the translation of the name *Menander*. The head of the expedition of the Greeks of Bactria went to the temple of Sankheyya, accompanied only by his lieutenant Demetrios. Nagasena was already there. He was sitting, surrounded by eighty thousand Buddhist monks. King Menander claimed to have managed, up to that day, to refute all the sophists who had been set against him in all the regions of India that he had conquered. 'The thinking of the Greeks,' he said, 'is the boldest of the known world. Even the Romans, when they were our conquerors, acknowledged its domination. This is why they send their children to Athens and to Alexandria to learn it.'

And this is why Milinda (Menander), when he arrived at the temple of Sankheyya, arrogantly whispered into the ear of his officer Devamantiya (Demetrios):

'Is this sophist even capable of discussing with me?'

Then, after looking at the eighty thousand monks surrounding the reverend Nagasena, the King of the Greeks added:

'What is this crowd that is pressing us? Thought is not an opinion. A single thought can be true against eighty thousand agreeing opinions.'

But Demetrios responded:

'My lord, this is not a crowd of people who think. These are disciples who learn.'

Whereupon, suddenly and for the first time, the King of the Greeks sensed something which, inside his skull, had begun to shudder. Here is the Pali text: 'Like an elephant hemmed in by a rhinoceros, like a naya hemmed in by garudas, like a jackal by boas, like a bear by buffalos, like a frog by a snake, like a snake by a snake charmer, like a demon by an exorcist, like a gazelle by the claws of a tiger, like a rat beneath the retractile claws of a cat, like the moon grasped between Rahu's jaws, like a bird striking the bars of a cage, like a fish beating against the mesh of a net, like a man who enters a forest and is frightened, alarmed, perplexed, nervous, all the flesh of whose brain begins to boil inside his bony skull, Menander's soul thought that it was possible that this sophist would triumph over the King of the Greeks by the end of day.'

CHAPTER 5

The Path of Thought

There is a kind of sobbing specific to the functioning of the mind and it makes blood flow from the nostrils.

Thought is related to death because there is a relationship between the return from predation to the hearth and the death that has been given far from the hearth, in the saltus, in the desert, in the ice field, in the outfield, in the jungle. There is a relationship within thought between the predator whom the hunter stalks and the dead prey that the priest cuts up, cooks, shares out hierarchically, and that the group—sanctified by the both unanimous and tiered number of its members—consumes.

Death, the rear base.

Once there is an intruder in the space, one either flees (horizontally, towards the horizon) or buries oneself (vertically, by rotation, in order to drill into the place itself and vanish into it).

In the past, one said (once upon a time, that is, back when wild animals spoke, that is, in the period of time when the human beings of Antiquity, still wholly covered with hair, were more often prey than predators, lived in trees, took refuge in mountain caves) that a cursed place could be discovered by sniffing (noesis).

From all these places of killing, an odour of ancient blood 'emanates' into space and 'remanates' into all the arts. This is Rembrandt's word for the faecal stench of his paint when those who had ordered one of his paintings had the bad idea of coming too close to his easel in his studio, in Amsterdam, on the third floor of a building located at the corner of Breestraat and the Zwanenburgwal. Nearing the window, one can still see the canal and Rabbi Menasseh's printing shop. Hunters who come close to art are at first overwhelmed by the rotten and nourishing and perilous stench of times past. When men and women are suddenly taken by a feeling of sickness that no cause explains, it is something that comes from death—from the instant that follows death, from consuming death, or from the bowels letting go in death—that they smell. This impression of confusion mixed with anxiety does not put forth whatsoever all the characteristics of fright or nausea. Adopting a state of alertness, springing forth, gripping, embracing that is itself still springing forth mortally, famished, hemming in, devouring—such is the noos (archaic thought). Such is the élan of thinking amid the carrion. The mind is a piece of living flesh that persists in living from its dead. Suddenly Jesus exclaims: 'Who has touched me?' A woman's fingers had squeezed the fringe of his cloak. Moreover, her bleeding stopped on the spot. On the spot, the originary blood stopped flowing once the woman's claws had touched the originary beast who persists in the god.

*

Look at the cats which slip outside into the garden, which reach the shore at dawn. Suddenly they sniff everywhere. Has a fellow creature gone by? Another animal? They search. They ask themselves a single question while they are wandering. Where is the Lord? They raise their eyes towards the still-nocturnal sky and look around. Actually, the Lord is not a question. The Lord is a place. The Lord is Dawn in the Place. Their little wet nostrils keep opening and closing on him as the darkness disintegrates.

*

Yagyu suddenly senses a sakki in the garden of his home while he is contemplating a cherry tree (because his page, who was coming up behind him to bring him his sabre, had thought that he could have easily killed his lord, by a single stab in his back, at that very moment).

*

The biter being bit. The first human figuration at Lascaux: the hunter killed by his prey. Such is the feeling of confusion, mixed with disquiet, in each body that devours to live, even before thought. This could happen. The inversion, at least the retroversion, the enantiodromia, is at the origin of the noesis.

A strange symmetry inhabits thought.

On an ancient Egyptian fresco, as on the Lascaux wall, the image still touches upon what is dreamt—*la rêvée*—prior to thought. Mice and rats take revenge out on the cat. They take it, with its four paws bound, onto a boat. A bird straddles it.

Symmetry is always aggressive. (In nature, symmetry is never a friendship between two heterogeneous entities but a mimetic craving between two living, devouring beings. In matter, likewise: an electric tension between two opposite poles.) In archaic thought, the argumentative reversion goes from prey to predator. In politics, it goes from the one whose throat has been cut to the cutthroat, from the one who has been absorbed to the eater, from the content to the container.

An Egyptian papyrus from the second millennium shows a General Mouse victorious over a cat pulled by dogs. This is how linguistic thought does not belie its origin in reverted natural images. Thought pursues the processes of what is dreamt. Thought pursues animal hallucination even when it believes that it has emancipated itself from it by clothing it in words. The question 'How to find one's path again?' covers a much vaster field than human space. It is about the return of insects to nests, fish to colonies, bees to hives. About the retrogression of all animals towards their lairs. The question 'How to find one's path again?' is immediately temporal: How to find one's mother in the present?' How to find again, among what is edible in front of one's eyes, what one loved in the past? What one drank back then? How to find the state of beforehand in the present?

The souls of humans, like the dietary tastes of all animals, are dominated by the figure of regression. Every desire returns to what is preferred. The compulsion of repetition is not inherently bad. Meta-phor in Greek expresses the same thing as trans-fer in Latin. The return to what is identical is the conatus itself. *It is vital to retrace one's footsteps.* It is good to devour with delight what one ate with happiness. The retrogressio is acquired at the same time as the migratio, because it is the same ex utero movement which founds the *ellipsis* (as spatial as it is temporal) and the regression (as temporal as it is spatial).

*

The movement of leaving ex utero constitutes the act of being born.

The extrauterine birth of viviparous animals predetermines thought.

Gnō means *connaître*—to be acquainted. This state of being acquainted with, this acquaintance or cognizance, comes from *naître*—the act of being born. It is the present perfect of the verb *naître*.

Being acquainted with means having been engendered. If being born means learning (*apprendre*), then having been born means knowing (*savoir*).

Movements of going and returning: such are, at first, the movements of being acquainted with and knowing.

Waves from before life on earth, which go out only to come back all the way to the place where the cliff collapses and invents sand.

Gignōskō means recognizing (*reconnaître*) a being by the sound of its voice, tracking down an animal by listening to its song, distinguishing a meteorological phenomenon by inspecting the shape of clouds or the direction of flights of birds across the sky. In Latin, gignōskō becomes cognosco. Cognomen is the sign of recognition. It is the proper noun par excellence. It is that which allows the singularity of a form to narrate its life. Every nickname is the trace of a silhouette in a field. Even narrare does not distance itself from being born. Narrating implies *engendering in detail the endlessly nascent*. Inenarrable means in-generable.

⁂

Thesis 1.

Thought keeps moving away in order to come back. In Greek vocabulary, this noos-nostos institutes the noetic relationship. In thought, the relationship itself constitutes the bond.

Scholium 1.

In Latin, the friendship of the natura naturata (the earth, the vegetation, the animals) for the natura naturans (the physical élan that drives them and the solar outpouring that feeds them and shines down on them) results from a dependence, characteristic of viviparous animals, of the content to the container (according to three modes: child to mother, recent to ancient, devourer to the devoured). Whence the adherence of thought to its exertion as a *temporal movement primed with a return*.

*

At Ephesus, Heraclitus had a haunting intuition that surpassed all his other ones. Language (logos) is this movement in the opposite direction (nostos in the journey, culpability in the psyche, boustrophedon in writing). Heraclitus invents the word 'enantiodromia' to indicate this movement, which he examines even in regard to his hand in the act of writing. The ploughshare of the plough goes from east to west, then from west to eat and then from east to west, endlessly.

The same is true of the writing of the sun in the sky.

He rebukes Homer for having said: 'May strife perish'.

There are no living beings without the irreducible difference between female and male, and only their face-to-face, and stomach-to-stomach, confrontation reproduces them. Harmony is the opposition whose violence is not interrupted. Living beings touch death every time they sleep. Once awake, human beings keep shaping the dreams in which their desire for other beings, which differ a little from them, directs them. Potters do not spin their wheels either in one direction or another; it is in both movements at the same time that the pot rises in their wet hands; in this way, potters imitate the rotation of the universe. The movement of the alphabetic writing of the Greeks is comparable to the potter's wheel in that the combination of the strokes of a few letters enables one to note down all the various objects and those that have disappeared in the past, as well as those that have never been seen and that will show their faces only in the future. Night and day are one. The screw, which is a mere curve followed by a curve, is straight. The rising road descends in the same way that the two slopes, one illumined, the other in shadow, form the same mountain. Life and death exchange their faces. He or she who completely forgets where the road leads keeps arriving in the original light.

*

In Greece, during the entire history of philosophy that has followed upon the life of the great Ephesian thinker (which followed upon his placing his book in the Temple of Wild Artemis before he left the world of human beings and fled into the mountains), sniffing and the scenting have called up, once they take place in the air, the odour of the past. In Greek terms: the noesis of the noos is nostos. Damaskios the Diadoxos—more than a thousand years after Heraclitus refused to be king at Ephesus—at the beginning of the sixth century, exiled no longer in Turkey but in Persia, continuing to write like the prince of Ephesus, in the same language, used the same words: 'For cognizance (noesis), as its name puts it, does not differ from the movement of thinking (noein). In this way, thought bears itself (neitai) and "goes back up" to Being. Thought is thus neoesis (it goes back up). If we call neoesis "noesis", it is by syneresis. The nous is epanodos (in our English terms: mind is a movement that goes forth while pushing life back to Being). The noesis (thinking) goes back up from zoe (animal life in the space of nature) all the way to the ousia (the *étance* or substance of Being in the depths of the sky among the stars).'

This is how, in Damascius' thought, the noetic quest *goes back up* towards the origin in the recapitulation of the development stages of the beings, from circle to circle, of animal life, of nature, of matter, of the cosmos.

On this point, the Platonists and the Stoics agree. Ontogenesis reproduces phylogenesis. The regression *goes back up*.

As one says of salmon when they *are* on the run back upstream, thought *is* on the run back upstream.

CHAPTER 6

On the Train Taking Poincaré to Coutances

Henri Poincaré: 'Upon arriving in Coutances and getting off the train, we got on an omnibus. At the moment when I placed my foot on the first iron step, the idea came to me, although nothing in my previous thoughts seemed to have prepared it.'

Rousseau was struck by a sudden inspiration, a genuine *vocal* inspiration, while reading in the *Mercure de France* the topic put forward by the Academy of Dijon. The turmoil of thinking at once emptied his soul and breathed into him a devastating voice in response. 'Just as I was reading, I saw another universe and I became another man.' He recalls the same memory, more than 20 years later, when he writes to Monsieur de Malesherbes, on 12 January 1762: 'If ever something resembled a *sudden inspiration . . .*' and he adds that his head was seized back then by a 'dizziness similar to drunkenness'. For 'more than four or five years,' Fabricius dislodged the ego from the depths of Rousseau's body. This is a transfer. This vertiginous, voluptuous transfer persists beyond writing, beyond the seasons. Plutarch's and Tacitus' hero settles for good in Rousseau's soul, like the demon in Socrates. Then like Socrates in Plato. Then like Plato in all the Neo-Platonists in the ancient world for a thousand years. This is how the movement of the transfer irradiates mental functioning.

*

The *excitatio* that rises during copulation *is* a meat-eating animal who springs forth and furiously attacks its prey. In the same way, an invisible fire suddenly sets fire to the whole organism of those who think.

*

When he discovered Epicurus' Greek oeuvre in Rome, Lucretius asserts, in *De rerum natura* 3.1, that he was struck by a 'joy of a sexual nature (voluptas) accompanied by shivering that had something divine (horror) about it'. It suddenly seemed to him that the 'walls of the world' (moenia mundi) drew apart (discedunt) in space like a door that opens on the surface of a wall and offers a vast view. This is how noetic raptures begin with a violent breaking up of the temporal continuity in whose rhythm a body recognizes itself. Then occurs an abandonment of self-control comparable to what is felt during spermatic ejaculation, or during psychic fainting after an emotion, or during psychic fainting while one is dancing or at the end of a trance. A loss of one's bearings that completely ravages the soul. Then, suddenly, the dazzling welcoming of another presence inside the self reorganizes everything.

The movement of thinking is a disarrangement which begins by making the soul struggle, and in which the rearrangement, suddenly ending it, becomes euphoric.

When Xenophon describes Socrates' ecstasy at Potidaea on the isthmus of Pallene, he calls it a *catalepsy*.

Plato in *Phaidrus* 242b describes Socrates in the same way that Suetonius will show Caesar coming to halt in front of the Rubicon: 'As I was going to cross a small stream, a signal (semeion) suddenly appeared in the air, and I stopped.' Here, it is a 'divine pause'. The voice of his demon says to him: 'Suspend all movement. Don't venture any farther.' So everything stops. At the edge of the bank, Socrates freezes. Caesar, on the bank of the little red river, Rubico, freezes. In each of us, everything, all at once, after having been entirely fragmented and disorganized, is polarized.

Plato's description is even more precise in *Ion* 533d: The body and the soul, in the strange temporal movement formed by this pause, are 'displaced, as happens with the stone that Euripides calls Magnetis and that most people call the Herakleian'. This specific hypnosis which goes beyond forms, from substance to substance, defines *magnetization*.

All these experiences that I am evoking and the descriptions that they offer imagine ancient content suddenly *relodged at the former address*. Spiralled up again inside the container. Re-involuted once again inside an anterior pouch.

Fundamentally, the magnetization of the beloved towards the magnet, the lover, towards he or she who loves (towards the erstwhile, towards she who loved, who was oneself) precedes parturition. This is why Socrates introduces himself as *maieutikos* (skilled in the art of midwifery) and does not hesitate to compare thought to a *maieuma* (a newborn) who leaves its mother to go towards the mother, to plunge once again its face in its mother's skirts, to grip them as if they were some more ancient fur, to die within the walls of the city.

Finally, Socrates borrows the image of strands of wool which enable one to bring content from one cup into another one. Thought is a transfusion, going from the form of a recipient to another form. Plato *Symposium* 175e: The fullest cup pours into the emptiest one through a strand of wool. But this transfusion movement is not restricted to the strand of wool that carries it out. Capillarity refers to the way sap rises in plants. Poros originally meant waterway, passageway. An aporia is therefore a deep drought, an aridity that waits to the extent that it attracts. An aporia functions inside the psyche like communicating vessels. Like hunger. Like thirst. Like desire. (Capillarity is bound to irrigation like enantiodromia is bound to ploughing. Both write on the earth.)

*

What force vanquishes gravity and suddenly sucks up hunger, thirst, desire into the siphons of the aporia? It is not air pressure that makes the liquid flow to the end of the pipe. It is the abrupt disequilibrium of the fluid itself. This sudden disproportion drives the metaphor (the transport of being to being). The same thing occurs in languages that engage transfers. Transport, synchrony and spring are bound together. Brought about by the disequilibrium of winter, all the sap rises all of a sudden, the she-bear comes out of her lair in the cave, all the leaves unfold one after another, all the flowers seem to blossom out together in a synchronization which fills one with wonder and which is the most beautiful spectacle offered by the earth to the eyes of those who live on it.

A spectacle that seems so beautiful to them only because they proceed from it.

They are thus born from it every year; they are *reborn* with it.

*

Finally, this instant of disequilibrium between the two forces set to work is *abrupt* and *sudden*. This champing or this suddenness characterizes the referent time. We might as well let it have its—marvellous—French name: *printemps*, spring. The French word *printemps* breaks down into the Latin *primum tempus*: the first time beat in the ordering of Time, the first step on which time bases its rotation on the earth, the originary time. This suddenness that strikes the first beat of the time measure in the soul or in the dance of time at the far end of space is the e-motio of the physis. The Latin word for emotion means e-movere, to go from, to move out from. The Greek word phusis means phuein, to surge. The French *Il fut* (it was) comes from the Latin 'Fuit'. The past tense of *Être* (Being) suddenly leaves the range of the verb einai (to be) and *tout à coup* (all of a sudden) resorts to the phuein. The Greek word exaiphnes (*tout à coup*, all of a sudden) defines this first 'beat' that marks the *prin-temps*: in the first beat struck by time in the natural year, *Être* (Being) leaves the *être* (the being) for the physis in the same way that the foetus leaves the mother to become a non-speaker (infans).

The god that Plato calls Exaiphnes (All of a Sudden, Sudden, Suddenly) indicates the temporal rupture between two existences. It is equivalent to birth among the viviparous animals.

It is the same case between two states of matter: when overflowing liquid lava during a volcanic eruption 'suddenly' (explosively) makes the field of cooled-down lava explode.

Between inner illumination and outer transfiguration.

Between two worlds: birth. (In this case, the strand of wool is the amniotic conduit.) An unpredictable surging forth that neither the midwife, nor the mother, nor the foetus can anticipate.

If this moment of impetus always reveals itself to be a 'sudden inflation', is it possible to distinguish the noetic experience from the ecstatic experience? Can one differentiate the shamanic trance from the sexual voluptuousness that it often mimics? And can the orgasmic instant be distinguished from the intracephalic spasm of drunkenness? And what about the dazzling flash from drugs? And the spiritual illumination that transforms, all of a sudden, the entire field of what one had thought up to then? An inspiration, a vocalization, which pressures the soul in an unexpected way, which searches, at all costs, for any piece of scratch paper so that the inspiration can be pondered and noted down? The imperious visitation of an image which obsesses one to the point of giving impetus to a recurrence? A rhythmic cell in which a song gradually begins to spin around itself? An oneiric sequence which readies itself to inch its way into the verbal sequence and to become contagious in the language? An image, a face, a 'muse' possessing one's body and binding the psyche in time, catching time off-guard? The immediate recognition of 'the other body' and the absolute attraction into 'another world' during love at first sight? The shivering beneath the skin or the aesthetic upheaval in front of such and such a site? The effusion of tears while listening by chance to such and such a recurrent vocal modality or while reading such and such a page that touches the heart? The trance which, after the whirling, incurves the body and projects it, with arms raised backwards, without the slightest precaution, towards the earth? The mystic ecstasy, strictly speaking, which also knocks over the body of he who is praying when whomever he is calling out to invades him, deploys him, modulates him, whereas it is the entire song in person which abruptly inundates him like a wave at the moment of reflux?

All these experiences have this in common: the metamorphosis is unvoluntary and the timing is unpredictable. The soul is as subjugated as the slave by the master—as the little child by the mother—and the body is more or less unconscious, displaced, inverted, 'outside of itself' as it was erstwhile at the moment of the e-motio when it exited 'outside of the mother'.

*

There is no identity (idem) in birth, nor of self in the soul of one who is born, nor even of proprioception in the volume of his or her body.

In the same way, there is no idem in love.

Plato wrote in *Phaidrus* 255c: The surging source that Zeus called desire (himeros) refers to the time when the god loved Ganymede. The flow surging forth from the body of the erastes gushed abundantly, with sudden abundance towards the eromenos, a part of it penetrating the beloved, but once Ganymede was full, the *rest* of this stream surging forth (rheuma) spilled outside.

There is an 'outside of the body' in love—both the body of the lover and the body of the beloved—which is like an *echo*: a splashing of desire comparable to the rebound of a voice against the wall of a cliff. The body immediately finds itself without a 'self', 'outside of the self', as it was *just before* being 'lunged' (just after the first world, where it lived in the other world of the other body). Being, having become again pure exteriority, projecting itself against the wall, *rebounds* towards the origin.

This 'outside of the body' that comes back onto the body are the wings that grow on the king's part (geras) of the body (the shoulders).

These wings are like vestiges of the overflowing into the Outside.

The rest of the flow of the Himeros.

This is how, in psychic life, it is as if thought were 'borne along by wings' and flies in the three worlds.

CHAPTER 7

Now I'll bring together the preceding theses, which have surged forth in disorderly fashion. Death emerges very early in thought. Perhaps even immediately. Thought is like a return among the dead. But death is there even earlier, prior to thought, in what is dreamt. A dream is a return of the dead who have been killed or devoured. Their images show them re-becoming killers or devourers at night; in any case, they are threatening. Hunger is the main problem of the body. Hunger extends its reign in space by means of death. Hunger consumes death. Hunger displaces, over the surface of the earth, each body that it constrains to move either in order to feed itself or to flee from a premature or brutal death. Around the head or muffle that moves forward, thought is initially a scenting, a sense of smell; the noos is initially a nostos; and the operation of thinking, the noesis, strives for the absolute return of that which it has scented among that which it scents. The depths of the body, in thought, seeking its sudden reunion with the lost object in the moment of impetus, in the unpredictable surging forth, in the 'suddenness' of birth, *runs* towards a kind of first time that it re-joins in the feeding-dying. Everything runs towards spring (*prin-temps*) and, behind spring, towards birth. When thought finds, the psyche is precisely, like spring during the year, an explosive, nutritive, expulsing, parturient, reproductive, ecstatic joy. The impression felt by the thinker is at first a sensation of reunion. Of re-budding. This is how I can begin, at the beginning of this book, by opening out the marvellous triptych of the three physical states in which noetic activity is carried out: as a joyous, voluptuous, or ecstatic activity.

*

Lucidity is the *joyous* state of the human brain. The exact vision. Neither a magnifying effect, nor the blurred vision of the long-sighted person, nor the warping of short-sightedness, nor a distant telescopic impression accompanies such joy. The good functioning of the organ is the first joy. Distinct vision, a panoramic lookout: lucidity is like a blue, aoristic, cloudless sky.

Its very depth turns the space, which it contemplates, blue.

And from the depths of the sky, light shines like water from a source flowing from the source. As it flows, it is clear, transparent, gushing forth, splashing, almost alive on the stones and among the roots and the flowers. This image of diaphanousness, of luminous clarity, shines throughout the works of Aristotle and Spinoza. It is the joy that Spinoza calls laetitia. It is knowledge of a third kind. As the ibex bounds from rock to rock, everything arrives beneath its feet in the right spot; the animal does not stagger; its hooves do not search for a support; it springs forth, it finds.

*

Voluptuousness refers to *sexual delight* in which the body loves itself to the extent of reproducing itself by spurting *outside* of itself. The moment of the ejaculation of semen is also a suddenness. It is the Aha that opens the Aha-Erlebnis. It the aorist of the Greeks in Eureka. It is a leftover from the death rattle that rises from the erstwhile. The short-circuit in the brain at the moment of the find is the sudden *re-notching* of the sexual organ in the other sexual organ. It is the origin, no longer as birth but as *conception* that drives thought. The Aha occurs following upon the tension, the effort, the research, the straining and the congestion in the strange muscle that inhabits the cavern of the skull. It is the solution—out of the blue—brought to a problem. It is the right word—or, rather, the *re-found* word—surging forth on the lips, ejaculating the meaning that it alone embodies. There is indeed a passionate voluptuousness that bloodies, that erects, that flows forth with signs. Alertness in the cortex, tumefaction of the soul, expansion towards the upper part of the upper part of the body. Abruptly setting the neurons on fire. One of Konrad Lorenz' pages describes the fever of a chimpanzee who suddenly discovers that a box can be used as a stepping stone to reach a bunch of bananas that he covets yet that his hand alone cannot grasp. A happy exaltation, before it induces his arms and leg to hoist himself, can be read on his face. Everything comes together at once (*d'un coup*), all of a sudden (*tout à coup*), in his eyes, as during the lightning 'bolt' (*coup*) of amorous recognition (*coup de foudre*). The chimpanzee's eyes open wide at the box, as when Argos the dog 'thought' Ulysses in the hideous beggar whom he spotted near the gate.

*

Finally, by the word *ecstasy*, I evoke all the possible short-circuits, both symbolic and de-symbolizing, even dissociating, however difficult they may be to qualify during the exertion of thinking. Breakdowns, heartbreaks, angers can also be ecstasies. One leaves reality. These are the semantic black holes of the inner world. Everything breaks apart all of a sudden, as in a nervous breakdown.

Content breaks through the wall.

Content suddenly saturates, overflows, devastates the cultural, acquired, linguistic or ritual experience.

Something from all that is exterior gets the better of the body.

This ek-stasis, which is specific to thinking, can be mortal.

When 20 years later Argos the dog recognizes the hunter in the beggar, his master in the hunter, his waiting in the arrival of the man, he dies.

King Redbad removes his foot from the world of the living, removes it from the baptismal vat, removes it from the paradisiacal promise, removes it from the affection of God, because he refuses to let his soul be converted to the required metamorphosis and, as he sinks into thinking about his dead ones, he breathes out his last breath through a *mouth become black*.

Thesis.

Our thoughts have content.

That thought has content means: one can die of thinking.

Redbad dies.

Argos dies.

There are two ways of dying of thinking.

1. One can die of thinking *noematically*. All martyrs die because of a thought. Tyrannicides expose themselves to the death that thus proves their thought. (Giordano Bruno burns on the field of flowers.)

2. One can die of thinking *noetically*. Suddenly the effort of thinking, the *noesis*, no longer leads to anything. (Marcel Granet in his study.) It gets stuck (Saint Thomas in the scriptorium).

CHAPTER 8

Marcel Granet's Death
during the Month of November 1940

Because he was a Jew, Marcel Mauss lost the right to preside over a French institution in German-occupied France. The position taken away from the great ethnologist and left open was taken over by Marcel Granet. He did so out of friendship for Marcel Mauss and with his assent. At the end of the month of November 1940, Marcel Granet went to Vichy. He returned to Paris, went home, pushed the door of his study, sat down at this desk, died. What could Mireaux and Carcopino have said to Granet? His mind was jammed. His soul was shocked. The anti-Jewish laws had been promulgated. Pétain had shaken Hitler's hand. Had a piece of knowledge worse than these loathsome laws been communicated to him? It is always possible that he had a *noema* that his brain could not include. The noema rerouted the noesis. There is ineffableness in the mind, itself a territory occupied from the age of 18 months by the national language and after having lived submerged in the vocal maternal emotion in which it was housed.

CHAPTER 9

Thomas Aquinas' Nervous Breakdown during the Month of December 1273

Thomas Aquinas is also sitting in front of his writing case. The greatest theologian of the Middle Ages is sitting in the scriptorium of the monastery exactly like the great sinologist Marcel Granet in his study, after returning from the station where he had gotten off the train from Vichy. He has his hand-sharpened goose-feather quill in his hand: the nib of the bird feather is full of ink; suddenly his hand lets go of the feather; he stops writing; it is the beginning of the month of December 1273. In front of him, his assistant, whose name is Raynaldus, lifts his eyes when, all of a sudden, the enormous, gigantic Doctor of the Church throws all his writing materials on the ground. Raynaldus immediately stands up. In fact, he does not really know what to do. He is distraught. He questions his master. Why has he just thrown parchment, quill ink and scraper on the ground?

'I can't stand it any more', says Saint Thomas.

The only thing that he added later (according to the *Vita* drafted by William of Tocco): 'It's straw.' (But this should be translated 'It's like straw' because Thomas Aquinas says in Latin: '*Sicut* palea') During this depression crisis, the greatest theologian of the Church thus still had the courage to forge an ultimate metaphor—culture conceived as something worthless, *like* a poor dried-up plant. Like hay. He considers the library surrounding him to be *like* a handful of straw. Then he no longer speaks. He leaves the *Summa Theologica* unfinished. This nervous breakdown, which will end in death, is a definitive depressurization of the noesis. It is no longer a noema (a content of thought) that blocks the brain. It is the noesis (the act of thinking) which no longer functions. Which empties itself out in space. Thomas Aquinas no longer writes, no longer thinks, no longer speaks, no longer contemplates, no longer prays, dies at the beginning of the month of March 1274.

*

Such is therefore the thesis that I want to examine inside this ninth volume of this last realm.

The little that we desire arduously awaits us farther on, unrecognizable, unthought-of.

The little that we can think surges forth like a beggar near a door, whom only the most ancient part of us recognizes, in any case stares hard at, if it has the courage to do so.

Thought scents space as in the sense of smell. Thought suspects. It grasps something of the world that is happening without retaining what has happened. We incessantly guide ourselves towards this 'little thing' which all of a sudden opens out in ecstasy (or which gets lost in the extreme, definitive ecstasy of death).

Moreover, in either case, it implies glancing at the abyss, aspiring to the abyss, dancing on the brink of the abyss.

I can add this surprising consequence: Ripeness defines the season when fragrances open out in the airs and head for their main predators. Age is the door to beauty.

CHAPTER 10

Introversive Trance

At the end of his life, Sandro Ferenczi asserted that the capacity to think was bound to a traumatic childhood event having verged on total psychic paralysis.

A good thinker is a human being who has experienced his brain in apnoea.

To express this in a Cartesian way: a 'thinking substance' (res cogitans) is that which has encountered the *void* inside of which it deployed itself. The intracephalic cavity must be represented as a big snail shell, with the substance that tightly fits inside its form having arrived by capillarity.

A fourth way of expressing this: The psyche which has experienced the danger of psychic death, not because it has survived the death but because it recovers, in a second period of time, its animal alertness, even if the latter has lost is originary modality—such is the rolling, revolving, circumvoluting movement that bears thought along.

To say this in a fifth way: Once the inner living world has been invaded by breath during birth, then by language during childhood, once it goes back over itself beginning with what it has lost, that is, once it *thinks*, it *com-pensates* for an aoristic abandonment. The body was confronted with this abandonment in a vital way at the instant when it first breathed, at the natal instant as it was leaving its mother. This is the great heartrending, amplifying, native void, itself lost inside the loss, leaving the Lost in space. The soul 'withholds' its breath in thought. This is why noetic functioning, in the depths of the solitary body, struggles by beginning everything again from the completely new breath (the Greek word psyche means breath) which is merely a secondary element with respect to the death that initially surges forth during birth. This is what inspiration means.

Initially, thinking fills a void. Even as every spring, year after year, is born from desolation, darkness, glaciation, desertification, winter. Thinking fills a head which has all of a sudden emptied itself out for ever, which has gone through mortal time, which has experienced nutritional deficiency or an emotional desert. Gradually thought chooses the intensity of the spasm, prefers noetic musculation and the noematic population to the terrible contemplation of that which it had to go through as an abyss (a loss, an abandonment, a void, a desert, a winter).

In human beings, thought characterizes the survivors among the living.

Every spring is a Survivor.

Thinkers—the survivors—are those who experience the need to start everything all over again at zero to understand what they have lived through. To retrace their footsteps and convoke witnesses. A thinker is a survivor who *comes back* into the world in which, however, he was born in times past and in which he has barely survived.

Even as his *pensation*—his thinking-ness—is a compensation, his prehension is a comprehension.

Bared intelligence depends on the degree of imminent death that the soul has neared.

Must thinkers be admired? No. An overinvestment of thought is the consequence of a proportioned traumatic disinvestment. Thesis 1. One should be wary of thought. The noetic is traumatophilic. *Thought likes what it is difficult to think of because the more it is difficult the less it has abandoned.*

*

The overinvestment of language by the one who was divested of it the most violently, or the most radically, or the most desperately, is of the same order.

It is in this second mode that thought has to do with literature.

Thought searches in the void with the language that the soul has acquired. But with literature, it is language itself that searches for itself, turning back on itself, empty of all content.

Nothing binds a human being with such force to his passion than the death from which he has escaped thanks to this passion. Yet because of this fact, this bond to death is indissoluble. The human being will not extricate himself from his wound with his knife—with his stylus. Confronted with the risk of psychic death, the thinker is a diver from Paestum who plunges into the Tyrrhenian Sea. He dives into a diachrony much greater than that which synchronizes what are called current events. He dives into a time greater than geographical space, into an anachronical abyss deeper than the historical sequence ordered around the moment when he is born until the daylight that comes in the following hour. Setting out from the traumatic chasm, he gets lost in that which is greater than himself. This 'world greater than himself' gets lost in a world as vast as the mother's uterus could be for the marula of the very first instants. The Lost—this is the object. The Loss—this is the call. Getting lost with the lost, this is what the verb meditate indicates: getting lost in the object.

Like Medeius in Medea (as when during meditation Medea's unborn child is lost forever in the waters of the pouch at the bottom of the stomach of his black Mother, Medea).

Hunger, which destroys with each manducation what it takes from the world, which loses again with each defecation what it has taken from the world, which endlessly empties itself out in order to become endlessly famished—such is the motor (motio) of predation.

The noesis is the only 'beyond' that predation has discovered for itself (whereas predation persists everywhere in a non-sublimated state: in commerce, in learning, in sexual desire, in marriage which associates relations and goods, in the transmission of languages, in the exchange and the fructification of money, in the unleashing of war, in rivalries for honours, in emulations of works, in competitions for salaries and positions, in power struggles).

✻

Does the evolutive identity take pleasure in noetic pleasure? Does the pronominal which is acquired during language learning abuse and comfort itself in the joy of its functioning? The brain copies the foetus. It is like a foetus in the foetus. Both arch in order to fold back onto themselves, in a morphologically similar way, the former in the cephalic cavity and the latter in the maternal pouch. The cerebral lobes and the foetus' body are both surrounded by water, both withheld by the membranes that envelop them, both hanging from cliffs. Brain and foetus are aquatic creatures absorbed by a body, turned upside-down, leaning towards the interior, hidden from daylight, protected from air. The brain is a foetus who is wary (to whom can be added fear, or at least vital alarm) and who remains at a distance. It is a living being who does not wish to expose itself in the visible world. The brain is the only organ of the human body that is insensitive to pain. Once the skull is opened, it is useless to fear the slightest suffering beneath the stylus that one points or the electrode that one puts forward. The brain is a mute being who wants to remain worthy of the destiny that it experiences in its silence. It is a wild animal who does not want to be born, who holds on, who does not yield, who does not flee the world in which it has been conceived and in which it dwells. It withdraws, it is insensitive, it concentrates, it remains alone, it isolates itself concentrically around its void, within the waiting that reigns in this void.

The nervous substance, the res cogitans, premature in time, remains partly free, in a state of freewheel functioning, digs into its refuge, persists in remaining mostly unassignable; beginning from itself (wherever it transports itself), the nervous substance opens a kind of space or spacing, a kind of angle, empty interval, free zone, unoccupied no-man's land.

The words 'no man' must be underscored in the expression 'no-man's land'.

Connections that are unoriented—non-instinctual, in-human, in-sensitive—perhaps make up what is specific to our strange species.

Our species is strange by dint of being premature at one end, unfinished at the other end.

A human being is an animal that is without genre, inhuman, without essence, without destiny.

*

Therefore, one must think while scenting. One must think while growing pale. One must think while being a little afraid of what is going to take place. Thought must be passionate for the person who discovers it as a surprising discovery. Thought must never cease being troubling, stressful, nervous, conflictual, traumatic, for otherwise thought is not in the process of thinking. As for the body, it suffers from the discovery made by the soul. An argument excites it—and overwhelms the former circuit and its habitual connections. Archimedes naked under the ashes experienced his thought as more explosive than the battle taking place during the siege of the city ramparts—or even more so than the volcano suddenly flaring up again above Syracuse and projecting its cloud of iron and sulphur onto the roofs and the walls.

*

In the intracephalic cavity, the starting up of the neurons knows no delay during the development of the brain. This is why *the recording of experience precedes birth*. This strange recording occurs without recursiveness, without any turning back on itself: the recording is not yet linguistic memory. A strange reel which turns without memory. The experimentation of life is by far anterior to breathing and this impression remains on the level of sensation. Listening to one's milieu is by far anterior to the possibility of human language.

Listening and living are anterior.

However, being born and thinking are exactly contemporaneous. Both come together in this way—neither in their conception, nor in their origin—but in the moment of nativity: as brothers-in-arms; as contemporaries of the loss.

Thinking consists of coming back behind oneself with the help of the acquired language in order to found anew, afresh, in an almost genital excitation for another life—with absolute linguistic freshness in an entirely new breath—the surging forth into the air.

During the birth of the body, the question of totality emerges at the heart of a being who is no longer the same. If there is a question of totality for the viviparous being who leaves the foetal state and the uterine world, it is that the totality is no longer there. And when the viviparous being enters the atmospheric world, and once the foetus has become infans, and then once the body discovers that it is gendered, indeed totality no longer exists at all. The being discovers reality.

Thesis 2. Retrospection. This totality, which is sensed as that which is no longer, means that it has been. Time emerges afterwards (and is consequently born out) in sexuation. Time is a scythe, a falx, a knife, a saxum, a sax. It is borne out like this: there is an inescapable erstwhile in the depths of the soul. There has 'been' a completeness. A pouch has 'been' watertight. Everyone has known fusion, in its silence, during the time of solitude. Its loss is the first atmospheric experience in everyone's pulmonary distress, in the act of being projected during parturition, in the fright sensed in front of an unknown world, in the threat of death, in the revelation of the sexual body, that is, sexed, sectioned, cut, culpable.

Thinking is set into motion by loss, even as hunger in the body is set into motion in order to devour, day after day, vegetation or dead animality, even as language truly *consumes* the *loss* of all the objects of the world that it has just designated, and this is why language, once acquired, will come to thinking as if magnetized by a kind of mourning similar to castration, to sexuation, to differentiation, to a bite: to biting remorse within each bite.

However, even as atmospheric life forms a body that is pulmonated, that speaks and is social, the foetal, emotional and solitary body has been formed by intrauterine life. Because there is an after-the-fact effect; there is a look-backwards. Because there is an ebb tide, there is this naked void and these shipwrecks rejected by the sea. There has 'been' a specific cabling for experience anterior to language and memory. There is what is prenatally cognitive. There is what is relational, what is umbilic; there has 'been' a world before the res cogitans ever on the lookout and more or less depressive. There is a strange skein of wet strands of yarn that are woven before sunrise and that make the worlds beforehand communicate among themselves. There is always a remote, solitary realm before society extends its domination. There have always been songs before the mother and an aphonic meditation before language.

*

Scholium 2.

Paradoxically, for a being who is born, the nature of ecstasy is introversive. The vessels communicate through the first void beckoning to the substance alongside it, which makes the substance rise in proportion to this void, proceed from it, come back, be exchanged. Despair, sadness, depression, all three of which are internal, offer the body the possibility of letting itself be invaded. The formidable loss that constitutes the desertic background of the atmospheric soul authorizes one to be swallowed up in the site that one is contemplating. In the same way, the desert, or the absence, which makes up the background of love, allows the other to take up a place that is unimaginable, considerable (greater than ipse and greater than ego) in the genuine nothingness of the abandoned soul.

CHAPTER 11

Sun

The flowers give off fragrance without having noses.

The sun shines without possessing a gaze.

Spoken language has no need of the consciousness that reflects it: in fact, it deludes itself in the reflection of an enigmatic body to which it gives names of death selected from the ancient stockpile of nicknames and patronymics of the genitors who have left the world.

For a long time, the functioning of spoken language has been mimetic, has been deprived of its own consciousness.

It happens that every movement in which we participate, when it causes no annoyance and provokes no pain, is imperceptible to us.

Nor do we perceive any more of the relationships which can be formed between bodies that move and those that do not transport themselves at the moment when the former progress at a comparable speed.

Thesis 1. Even as times past are forgotten in the living world and even as we inherit from its evolution without our having participated in it, we lose the memory of having once painfully learnt the organization and the lexicon of the language that we speak at the instant when we think.

What is dreamt persists in the depths of thought and, there, it does not completely forget the sleep that had offered it to the skull, but it does not perceive it. For thinking is also a kind of sleep. It perceives only the missing objects that its dream brings back in the form of mendacious images.

The imagination is deeper and more insistent than all the symbols, oppositions, divisions, languages, roles, signs.

Thought goes wherever it wishes in a dream, in the same way that death strikes wherever it wishes in nature in order to nurture life and extend it.

*

Scholium 1. If puerile life, of a linguistic nature, is a memory that lasts for an entire lifetime, then foetal life is not of the order of reminiscence. Intracervical life will always be anterior to the memory that language fabricates while procuring landmarks for it. The condition within *in utero* life is the structure of the structure. It is like its sleep in the process of always dreaming. The setting up of the network is immemor. A being is memorable, *sub sole*, only if, having learnt to speak, he inscribes traces while speaking in the second world, distinguishes them by naming them and harmonizes them with his light. Myths respond to the same vital need as the dreams preceding them. The images of tales accomplish desires that words, just acquired from the terrifying or sarcastic lips of the those who teach them, are afraid to designate in ordinary life. Oneiric sequences preform the bewitching intrigues that hallucinate solutions from frustrations in the same way that tragedies set in motion the ecstasies which, removing the pain of carrying out the act, perhaps present a cathartic character, and, in any case, assign to the soul an oneiric model that defies it. Myths, tragedies, speeches, phantasms and dreams endlessly tell lies and are endlessly prolonged like newborn beings falling into the world. Every soul—even that of a killer, a philosopher, a saint, a prophet, a son of God, a thief—looks back on itself and copes with its fairy tales while preparing its murder, while polishing its argument, while constructing the dimension of its martyrdom, while carrying out its images in the enigmatic order in which they have come to him before revelling in all his dead ones who hail all his memories.

*

Scholium 2. The first cry rises with the abandonment of the host body.

Everything that is said while pushing out one's first breath is above all a farewell.

Also, everything that one will be able to say in the language that one learns in the light will above all signify this farewell made to an anterior, internal, withdrawn, secret, non-luminous, solitary realm of sound but not of speaking.

Chronos immediately devours those whom he engenders once they have been expulsed into the light and he discovers them there.

The god Time will devour all living beings separated among themselves by the projection of light in the visible world and set in opposition to each other by sexuality so that they can be renewed.

And the sun will go out and space will devour itself, and, as it devours itself, it will devour the time in which space has deployed itself, will devour the earth, will devour the memory of animals and of human beings and of dreams and of words.

The memory of death itself will disappear during the night when all human languages will be reabsorbed at the same time as the breaths that addressed them to the astral wind blowing by.

CHAPTER 12

Ariadne's Thread

A tree trunk. A rocky ridge. A blind spot in regard to other predators. Inside this angle one bends one's legs, settles oneself in, fits oneself in, buttresses oneself, huddles up and watches. One looks out vacantly, sheltered, but one looks out. Even reading looks out. Surveillance, malevolence—such is the state of being on the lookout which remains withdrawn in the depths of thought; it withdraws further; it retracts further; it thinks only of springing to kill since hunger has hollowed out its body and ecstasied its watching until it dreams of prey in the forms surrounding it.

In Greek, if the word 'nous' (mind) comes from the word 'noos' (smell), this first sniff in the air is born at the dissimulated place where one once again dissimulates one's body in the external space, where one dissimulates one's thought, where one keeps secret what the body is going to do—before throwing oneself at top speed on one's past passing by.

Of course, wild animals, like hunters, also have a noos, an angle, a nook from which to concentrate on that which they are in the process of scenting, a retreat, a front, a cave, a shelter, a hideout, from which will suddenly surge forth the unpredictable aggression.

Alcman, fragment 55: Who can express the noos of another being? The tiger's noos: the tiger's project and its lair? Who can express the thought of a bird? The flight of the bird of prey circling around its nest like a spinning top and dancing in the sky by spreading out its strange feathered arms? Hiding its beak, its talons, its egg, its nest, at the highest place in the world, at the steepest point where the earth stands upright into the sky? Who can make reason out of the leaving and returning of the spotted panther, which never takes the same path in nature? And what is there inside what one might call the 'erectile' head of the meerkat which suddenly comes to a halt, raising its head higher, its neck stretching up above its collar, and turning its gaze in the air like an absolute sentinel? What is there inside the bony cephalic cavern of animals in which the same hunger incurves and hollows out, in which the same desire withdraws and buttresses itself? What is this wild-animal thinking that competes with human thinking? How can this noos—which perks up its ears, that is, which turns and coordinates its two ears towards the slightest deviation, in sound, in the prelinguistic world—be defined more precisely?

Perking up one's ears is to the soundwaves of the world what sniffing is to the air that passes by and to the odours that it bears along.

Two traces persist, in ~800, in Homer's songs. In the *Iliad* 15.509, Homer wrote: There is no better *noos* than a body-to-body combat with the enemy. (Thought is a body-to-body combat between two 'differents'. There is no better thought than throwing oneself onto that which one desires, that is, the polarized assault, sexual coition, the mortal duel.) Later, in Turkey, Heraclitus re-examined Homer's text. But Homer is the only writer to specify, in the *Iliad* 15.80, a little higher up in the song that he composes—the temporality specific to this connective springing forth: Hera is *as swift* in the sky as, on the earth, the noos of a man day-dreaming inside his lungs. Such is the dimension specific to Exaiphnes, the god of Everything-All-of-a-Sudden, the demon of thought. This demon of Suddenness is the god of the re-betrothment of time frames. Not the matching up of time frames, but of the short-circuit of time frames. Thought, while it is thinking, while it is com-pensating, thinks that it re-finds 'itself' in the traumatic places from which it surged forth in times past. This is symbolization in action.

Martial evokes stags who crash their antlers against each other, embedding themselves in each other, dancing, stabbing each other without yielding an inch of ground, and falling, in autumn, skewered. Symmetrically positioned with respect to each other, they breathe their last breath into the mist at the same time. They frustrate both the panting dogs surging forth among the dead leaves and the black ferns, and the hunters who have followed their tracks and now arrive running with spears in their hands.

The noesis speeds to the source where it can nourish itself. It swoops down like a bird of prey; it swoops down like a metaphor; and as a metaphor, it leaps from body to body; every silhouette is its approximative prey. All at once, there is the lookout, the prey, the springing forth of the hunt, the jutting out of sexual coition, the assaulting of the warrior-like assault. At once the hide-and-go-seek in the forest and the putting to death in the extraordinarily sudden capture. The black Mother stands behind thought even as the Lost stands behind the body that appears in this world. This is why each body that appears in this world is its vestige. Even as the wild animal is behind the track that it has left on the ground without thinking about it. The Lost is the Siren in whom is mixed, moreover, old shells, old feathers, great wings opened wide to envelop the feminine, soprano, soothing, luring song. In the Greek word seiren, seir means 'to bind'. The siren is the maternal bond in person: the cloth strips of the swaddling clothes following the knotted umbilical cord. The word 'seira' defined the 'lasso' for the Scythians. Thought is this singular lost voice that binds to each other the absent, the deceased, the traces, the excrements, the vestiges, the impressions, the memories, the images. The act of thinking is this 'emotion' that transfers all the names which were borne by the dead and all the words which were pronounced by the dead onto the faces and lips of the living. Even as re-liaison presupposes liaison, thought presupposes the *lieuse* (binderess): the Siren, the Great Mother of fecundity, and Hera, the goddess of all women. Even more ancient, she who presides over deliveries of babies, she who is the mistress of all animals, the goddess of the mountain and the forest: Artemis the Huntress, in whose temple Heraclitus, Hera's servant, refusing the realm of Ephesus, deposited his book before fleeing into the mountains, a deer among deer, perking his ears among the animals perking their ears, pursued by barking dogs and children throwing stones at him.

*

Ariadne—this strand of wool between man and beast—says to the man: 'I give you a thread as a guide.'

Ariadne then gave Theseus a ball of yarn so that he would survive in Daedalus' daedal maze.

Dedi pro duce fila. I have given you a thread as a guide.

I have given you, for a duc, a piece of thread, a bit of umbilicus.

The way in which the Greek hero uses this thread must be examined more closely. Anticipating a 'no return' from the labyrinth which leads from the human world to the wild natural world, Theseus ties the thread to the door of the inextricable network of paths that Daedalus the architect has conceived. For King Minos had asked Daedalus to come to Crete in order to build a prison with *no way out* to lock up the half-man-half-beast whom he had had to recognize as his son. Theseus progresses prudently by unwinding Ariadne's thread without breaking it inside the maze of the different stages that go from the human world to the animal world (phylogenesis). He arrives at the stable where the bull lodges, watches out for it, springs forth, faces it, kills it. Then Theseus winds back up the thread into the shape of a skein, pulling gently on the thread to find 'the door that no other mortal before him had ever found again' (ontogenesis).

※

Learning a language by one who doesn't speak proves that the acquisition of a language is not intentional. A 'consciousness' is lent by the mother to her infant in the sense that it is presupposed to be in him. The mother invents a comprehension in the infant to whom she constantly speaks, gradually leading him, with no return, into the language that he doesn't know.

The cum, in cum-prehensio, is *comme* ('as' or 'like'); the mother speaks to the little one 'as' (*comme*) if he were human; this is how the *comme* of a comparison (of the metaphora) is the transfer.

The mother uses the *Tu* infinitely before dressing it in the language that she subsequently constructs in him, during a period of five, six, seven years.

This *tu* is like a thread, which goes from her to him, which makes of him an ego (18 months later) that goes from him to her.

But this original non-consciousness never becomes conscious of itself (except in a loss of language that prohibits it). It is no longer Granet dying, but Benveniste dying. Pure premonition of the returning-to-retaining-from the envelope (skin, medium, nest, book) which preserves the individual in his milieu. If, according to philosophers, the conscious-of is assured in the object, I seek to think an unassured, non-objectal, non-present, non-ego, non-idem pre-intentionality which progresses, which awaits protrusively and sexually, which goes from the door to the stable and from the stable to the door.

Which goes from the manure heap to the gate.

Which drags the dead to the living.

*

The hands–mouth–gaze complex is the first explorative, eroticized triad. As in love, the hands–mouth–gaze complex seeks fingers-lips-eyes. Seeks to grasp together. To be absorbed in the capture.

Cum-prehensio.

The thinker's body is the body of a predator at the moment of his predation, even in the absence of a visible, graspable, devourable prey.

However, he does not spring forth, he does not devour, he does not close down his jaws on something. Even as a dream sees what is not there, a word pronounces what it does not grasp.

*

Meaning is a 'sentiment of comprehending' which *distances itself* from the capture that it anticipates. It suffices to antici- pate it. Suddenly putting a hand on the thing stops the grasping. Approaching suffices. So strong is the bond.

Zeno showed his open hand with his fingers almost whitened by dint of being stretched out. 'This is representation', he said to his disciples.

He slightly contracted his fingers. 'This is assent.'

He closed his fist. 'This is comprehension.'

Then he moved his left hand forward, tightly grasped the right fist with his left hand to the extent of forming only a single ball of fingers. 'This is science.'

So many prehensions, so many predations. One must com-prehend what is to be com-prehended. First, the living being freed his hands and raised his face, then he thrust out his claws into nature and closed his fingers around the object. Subsequently the soul lost both fingers and things in language. Everything is forgotten of what constantly persists, even as our bodies forget the scene of which they are the vestiges. This is what Cicero wrote in *Prima Academica* 2.47.

*

Even more simply, Ovid writes in *Metamorphoses* 8.137: filo relecto.

Theseus progresses *filo relecto*. Relegere, rewind the thread, rebind, reread endlessly, retie endlessly the words to the reality preceding them, replunge endlessly the logos into the physis. Replunge the face into the grass that it gnaws at. Never lose sight of the more ancient silent abyss of the origin.

Rebound by the rereading *filo relecto*. Living on the thread of reading.

My life, comprehending nothing of anything, seeking to progress, to be reborn incessantly, to comprehend. Vita via filo relecto. My life living and reliving along the endless thread of rereading.

CHAPTER 13

Ariadne's Death

Holding his skein of thread in his hand, Theseus didn't inform her and followed the shore.

He followed the edge of the shore that touched the water as if it were a thread.

He returned to his boat. He went aboard. He grasped the rope with both hands. He abruptly pulled on the rope. He hoisted the sail. He departed.

This is how, without saying anything to her, without looking back, Theseus abandons Ariadne, clinging to an isolated reef among the seals and the wolves. She raises her eyes; sea hawks are flying over her. She is on Dia Island, across from Gnosis. There, on her rock, as she cries out more and more in vain, as she shouts less and less loudly, the name of Theseus who has left her behind, as she dies on the spot where she has been left behind, as she moans this beloved name softly, woefully, hauntingly, the name gradually becomes a song and ceases to refer to a human being, while she modulates and accentuates her threnody in her pain, it is *Liber* who comes to take her in his arms, who opens his wings and transfers her into the sky.

CHAPTER 14

The Boomerang

On the signs that captivate thought and prevail over the emotions of the soul. We belong to a species that prefers thought to recognition (in Greek: where the noesis supplants the agnorisis), for we proceed from a (human) genre and from an (animal) realm in which predation entirely dominated contemplation.

In the *Iliad* 10.466, Homer simply wrote: A path is the tamarisk branch that one breaks.

The semata are initially markers left on an odos. Zurück. Signs are initially signals enabling one to find one's path during wandering quest. In Greek, the ode is a tale that is a path. In Chinese, the tao is the way that expresses and does not express beings. As much as it is difficult to distinguish going from coming back, it is difficult to differentiate between path and tale, and to discriminate between the signifier and signified. In Greek, markers were called gnorismata, then they became symbola. In Latin, these identifiers were first called crepundia before they became signa.

*

Scholium. We are a species that not only preferred being on the lookout to seeing, but we are a species that envied all the urges of all the other beings wandering across the surface of the world. As omnivores, we ate everything while running the risk of perishing, making use of whatever was at hand, making a survival out of all forms, making a transfer out of any metaphor. One desired and one tested. If a 'test' now indicates an examination, with an identical task, to which a human group is subjected in order to hierarchize the best among the group, in times past the word 'testa', which lies in the depths of test, meant the sawed skull whose bony cavity was used as a recipient (for thought as for the originary alcohol, by intertwining notions or experiences, by blending ingredients or ferments).

Headstrong head.

If nothing is contemplable without active destruction (the death of the prey brought to our mouth) or passive destruction (our death in the teeth of the prey become our predator), if nothing is theoretical if not the remains of that which was eaten by the notching together of both jaws, then the noetic completely blends into the verb noein. I sense blood. Therefore scalp, head, skull, wood, bone, horns, teeth, fur, feathers become primordial signs once again. The watchdog of the dead inhabits the return (nostos) thanks to his sense of smell (noos). With their virtuoso noses, dogs know this return better than human beings can ever manage to learn it. Human beings, influenced by wolves, gather into packs. We are always the domesticated beings of those whom we are proud to have tamed. The Other is put into our inner oven before we are. We eat.

Horses are also the greatest noeticizers because they are the fastest. Galloping at top speed, they come from the world of the dead. They escort back there, more woefully, in a more trotting way, more slowly, pulling hearses. After horses, I no longer dare to name turtles and their islands, salmon and their sources, birds and their infinite migrations, from continent to continent, the continents themselves from sea to sea, searching for a sea that was but a sea. Strange circuits in Being that are preceded in the planets around the stars and in the stars within galaxies exploding and burning endlessly in the sky that they illumine by means of the *propagation of their memory.*

Black swifts not only come back to the place where they were born. They return to their cave and, in their cave, to the nest in which their shell was broken open.

*

In Greek, the word palintropos means the path which really returns. The being which really returns is the thrusting stick called a boomerang. For Heraclitus, enantiodromia—as for Parmenides palintropy, as for Ulysses palinody—is the path that defines the human being. Palintropos means retrovision. In German, this is Zurück. Palinody defines the path of the sun to the solstice. It is the nostalgia specific to the physis, to the place where the Mother of the sky takes action. The rectilinear movement of the straight line turns back or the elliptic movement of the circle makes a loop. This, then, is the German word Rückblick. It is an urge to go and see what it is that *flows back* to the origin, towards the hearth of the mothers, towards the lunar metamorphosis of the seasons. Then the cycle of the seasons becomes the narration of the events that populate them. For having someone in thought is quite simply remembering him in language. Even as the sense of smell awaits a living presence, once it has a premonition of it. Even as eyes on the lookout and watching in all directions are attentive to an unexpected form that might surge forth. Being on the lookout, for the soul, is an absolute 'awaiting'. In the same way that the Greek word noos is already in the word nostos, the French word *gard* (guard) is already in the word *regard* (gaze, watching). Artemis 'guards' the source at the heart of the wilderness where she delivers her mother of her twin brother, Apollo. And the twin is the son of her own twin sister. The same happens to all the words formed in any language. Once again, Heraclitus writes: Palintropos harmonie—in regard to both the bow and the lyre. The bowstring and the lyre strings exert a traction on the wood which itself receives each string and stretches it. It is this double traction, in both directions, which creates the beauty of the sound when the beauty of the sound expresses nothing other than the precision of the death from the arrow that speeds towards the prey.

Neuron refers to the bowstring. This string is like the thread on which Theseus pulled to come back.

That which is neuronal extends axons and dendrites in the volume of the still-closed skull.

Noetic is relative to the act of putting oneself in the spirit of *out* and of going in turn from the *in* towards the *out* and from the *out* to the *in*. Scenting. Eating. Tasting. Becoming acquainted with.

82

Noematic is relative to that which one has in mind, the *out* which has flowed back into the *in* and which is dissolved there. Digesting. Knowing.

Nostos is returning in the sense of *going from where one has left*. This active nostalgia is less the return of bees to the hive as the *positional* dance of the prey found directly below the stars in the sky.

*

Montaigne: Ever since Antiquity, scholars have pillaged and foraged books as bees do with the flowers covering the fields.

Reading was itself preceded, for millennia, by enquiry on the tracks of prey fleeing an approach to escape from mortal combat.

In the same way that our body is the vestige of an absent body, in the same way that images silhouette a body that is no longer, in the same way that names call a body that is not there, in the same way that tracks indicate a missing body.

Thesis 1. The hunter is *first of all* a reader.

Thesis 2. From this, it follows that the tracks are *already* letters. To say this in Greek, however unequal noesis and anagnosis are in the mores and passions of human beings, they are bound. *Thought* and *reading* enchain each other in turn. They compete. Curiositas (the capacity to say *cur*, the aptitude to ask why of each being and of each thing) is incessantly led around by the nose of this sniffing nose, by the anxiety of this suspecting scenting, by this peaceless quest. This is how curiosity is bound to a pleasure of abandoning oneself endlessly, like a running dog, to a demand that will never be satisfied.

The curiositas impassions the soul with a desire that experiences no de-excitation following upon its pleasure.

Thesis 3. This is why study is the most beautiful of gifts.

*

When Plotinus writes 'the mind is unaware that it is contemplating itself', does he simply mean that, in the Greek word 'nous', what is left over from the 'noos' contemplates in itself the 'nostos'? Does he mean that in the soul, intelligence adores reading? Does he mean that inside the head, attentiveness is on the lookout only for the recapitulation of lost joys, preserving it in nocturnal hallucination, in unaccomplished desire, or at least in the excitation that is constantly unappeased until the genital age, which remains near the origin like its twin brother? Are reader and thinker brothers like Sleep and Death? Or, instead, doesn't thought contemplate the Lost in itself? The invisible at its source? The mistress of animals? Diana goddess of Ephesus? God himself—in the world of 'catholic' Christians—when the latter desired to relay the 'universal' (*kath'holon*) fire of the Stoics of ancient Rome? Isn't the Ersatz of dream, par excellence, the beloved absent one?

But Plotinus continues: In this state, the soul thinks not even of God because it doesn't think any more at all.

Such is prayer. Prayer is the act of thinking which lacks all content. It is noesis without noema. It is the mute voice (in Greek, this 'mute' is called 'mystic') of the inner world. An invocation without an addressee. A signifier without the signified.

According to Plotinus, extreme thought defines prayer.

And it is possible, in fact, that the *cur* rests there in its erstwhile.

*

Zhuang Zhou (Zhuang Zhou is the name of that shaman who lived in the forest, in the province of Henan, in the same period of time when Heraclitus, on the Turkish coast, climbed the hill that loomed above the temple of the huntress goddess of Ephesus) wrote: Thought is a journey that crosses the world. Once the body falls backwards, the soul flies off to make its visual round trip. Such is the celestial tao of the souls of shamans. The same is true of theories and dreams. The same is true of the thoughts of human beings and the hallucinations provoked by mushroom smoke or by alcoholized honey, rice, grapes or maize. The return of the shaman is a carmen, an ode, a tao, a path, a voice that meticulously modulates its itinerary. This song or chant that hails it or this rhythm that is beat out on a drum, to situate the earth in space, brings the soul back near the body. The return has become a song or chant (odos) that expresses the path (odos) or, rather, a dance that displays it. This is how bees do it. Such is the tao of honey in the origin. In the verb 'neomai', the revenant bees dance their 'revenance', their return; they do not weep over the vanished flowers; they *situate* the bush in the site. They pass on its position to the other worker bees. This dance that goes back over is called a 'theorem' in the Greek language.

CHAPTER 15

Theoretic and Cynegetic

What is a hunt? A hunt is a hunger that gathers its paws beneath itself, that retracts its claws, that hollows out, calms down, waits patiently, organizes itself before it sets out to capture with the best chances possible. Gathering itself together. Retractility. Every noetic has been contained in the primal cynegetics. The *reflexion* of death before the springing forth is entirely contained in the *re-flexion* of the hock during the surging forth of the body from its hideout, or from its bush, or from its blind spot, at the instant of the assault. If hunger is the primary cura, curiosity (hunger without hunger) is secondary; it belongs to a second time phase. Curiosity reveals an ancient viviparous content extending forepaws, the senses, the eyes and memories towards a container that has become invisible in space. The whole body is curiosity even before the soul begins its sojourn inside it. Any desire is this tension before the sexual embrace. The whole body is already prayer. On the one hand, in space, predation scents, wanders, springs forth, grasps with its teeth what can be devoured. On the other hand, the regression in time—desire, dream, language, memory—seeks to re-join the anterior state, goes back to what is preferred, wishes to restore—in the depths of the body—the satiety of the first world, desires to resuscitate the sexual voluptuousness of the conception.

Corollary 1. All rhetorical figures, without exception, derive from hunting tricks and disseminate them.

Corollary 2. All hunting tricks, all war strategies, all rhetorical figures, in brief, all death tactics, are undifferentiated.

*

Cercher—to search, to seek—was long used in our language. The Latin verb *circare* meant to go around, to turn around. This is how birds of prey 'search' in the sky. Suddenly they encircle a point straight down below, which is what will become their prey. They drop down like a line that their body traces in the air that they cut through. The bird then looks like a stone falling vertically. That drops straight down.

In English, *to search* derives from the Old French *cercher*, to wander in a circle, to roam in a circle like planets around stars or little children around their mother.

*

A dream is itself a hunt for what has been lost. Motivity is impeded, but movement is perceived. The paratactic articulation of its sequences is a hunt. A linguistic narrative is also a hunt. A sentence is a hunt. In Latin, each narratio, transforming scattered acta into a consecutio of stages, is explained as a venatio.

There are five stages: hunger, prey, predation followed by death, manducation.

Five stages: a lack which hollows out the solitary body, desire that erects it, ordeals that it overcomes in the putting to death, mourning followed by a wedding banquet that satiates. Such is the universal schema concealed beneath the plan. There are two nuclear functions specific to any narrative: Propp's two theses: 1. Lack, assigned task, accomplished task, plenitude. 2. Plenitude, interdiction, transgression, lack. To the extent that these two functions retrace their steps, they form a single function whose *palinodic* nature and *retrospective* reading must be pondered. For, when one says that narrative (in Greek, diegesis) is a hunt, one initially means that the succession of its stages is not a meaning but a trap. A common noun searches for an adjective. To the victor is attributed an attribute. A subject demands a predicate. If the hero already possesses a *nom* (name), then he is 'renamed' and obtains *renom* (renown). Alke (Alcaeus) becomes Herakles (Heracles). Strength (in Greek, alke) becomes punishment for the violence (of the rape), a punishment that the goddess Hera divides into 12 successive labours, at once wearing down the hero's strength by sub-dividing it into the distinct chapters that compose the legend covering him with glory (kles).

*

At the end of the narrative, the princess is liberated. She becomes a woman. She contemplates her savoir who has spared neither his strength nor his tricks. She asks him who he is. But often the hero remains silent, or does not avow his name. (Jan de l'Ors does not say that he is a bear.) He responds:

'I am two.' (I am the double man.)

A shaman is the double man, even as an initiate is a duplicated man, even as a reader is a man of two worlds.

He who has gone away and come back is the *survivor*.

The victor is always the *enantiodromos*, he who is an animal for animals and a human being for human beings, the predator who becomes the prey, even as the prey once again becomes the predator.

These are *Metamorphoses*.

Plato speaks of a 'hunt for reality' in *Phaedo* 66c.

Plato speaks of a 'hunt for beauty' in *Protagoras* 309a and in *Symposium* 217a.

Aristotle speaks of a 'hunt for happiness' in *Politics* 7.1328b1.

Nicholas of Cues speaks of 'venatio sapientiae', even as Montaigne speaks of 'chasse de cognoissance' as a way of characterizing study.

*

Intellectual curiosity is, at first, entirely contained in the lookout that is on the lookout for the lookout of the wild animal that is on the lookout. This emulation makes up the heart of research. The depth of theory is enantiodromic. What applies to you applies to the other, and what applies to him applies to you. This curiosity about the curiosity of the other is originarily impassioned because it is vital: famished, avid, impatient, excited, gourmand, exultant. It is the putting to death of the predator that has become a prey which founds the guilt specific to the prey that has stolen the predation from the predator. This reversion forms the basis of all reflexion. Its nature is always temporal. For millennia, the hunter was wholly on the lookout for what was passing in front of eyes both desirous and ruthless because they were famished. The passer-by of the human past has nothing human about it: it is always an animal. Such are the wild animals recorded on cave walls, seasonal relays, annual solstices that come back—twice, or four times, or twelve times—over their own passages. It is a hunger or a desire that is suspended and that spies on reality to discover what it searches for in a way that is as necessary as it is famished and as famished as it is recursive. Pasts that pass back over their past passages. In the ancient Japanese world, life is deeply and magnificently this: pasts that pass back over their past passages. Mortal haste is expressed in two manners. In the field of the contemplatable, a human being is pressured by death twice: in the centre and at a distance. By inner death (dying of hunger), by outer death (being devoured by the hunger of predators or by vultures).

CHAPTER 16

Fundamental Noetics

Five strategies have gradually emerged from this ante-human fascination for human prey subjugated by their predators' haunting, ever-threatening, often triumphant gazes.

The *affût*—the lookout, the blind—consisted of waiting motionless and out of sight from those gazes, upwind from those senses of smell, near a habitual passageway, a gorge, a watering hole, at the bottom of a cliff. The *affût* is solitary. It is silent. It becomes immobile. It becomes invisible. It blends into the landscape. To the *affût* can be added camouflage, then disguise, a mask, the lure that the animals themselves teach. Before animals, plant life sets up its own first lures within what is visible, that is, before even the arrival of the wild beasts that the vegetation will lure so that they will reproduce it by transporting seeds. Among animals, in the cruel gorge of beauty, the master of the *affût* is doubtlessly the anglerfish which keeps its extraordinary dark mouth open in the shadowy depths of the water.

The *poursuite*—pursuit, chase—aspired to force the prey into the imitation of its course. The inherence that the pursuit inscribes in time and space in the form of speed can be a solo, a duo, a trio, a quartet. This is how the tempos of the 'suite' are like the movements of the music-dance. The *poursuite* is the prodigious dance that results from the springing forth of death. The master of the accelerated *poursuite* is the lioness or the tiger or the jaguar.

The *rabattage*—driving—consists of the first collective offensive predation. The pack surges forth with it. Hunting in packs was taught to human beings by wolves, whose cries are as consonant with languages as plaints resemble their howls. This is how wolf societies and human societies assembled and inter-domesticated themselves. Hunting in packs engenders human society. This collective hunt divides society into two clearly hierarchized groups. Those who push back wild animals by scaring them, by driving them violently, by smoking them out, by barking, by vociferating, by drumming, by making a lot of hellish noise. Those who wait for them, motionlessly, silently, with one knee on the ground, pointing their spears, or preparing their stones, and who put the animals to death in a dead end, at the back of a cave, at the bottom of a cliff, or with nets placed in a funnel. Human hunting society is always based on at least two opposing communities that inequitably group together against a third party. The secret of these societies is the invention of the enemy—who is as unreal in space as the line at the horizon of the sky or the border at the limit of a country. The great master of packs is the grey wolf, who came from the east, humanized itself in a fairy-tale-like way into a deeply moving dog, almost more human than human. 'Homo lupus homini' means: man is a domestic dog in the war packs whose cries (languages) define nations.

The *piégeage*—trapping—indicates a predation that is carried out in ever more ingenious, technophilic, technophoric, fate-less, progressive, artificial, cumulative, interminable ways. The traps go back to techniques imitated from many animal habits. Snares, branch-formed funnels, enclosures, nets, whistles, calls, glues, electrical charges, poisons, etc. Before entirely artificial traps, more natural traps were selected. Swamps in which legs, hooves, claws would get stuck; gorges in which flocks, herds, packs would be enclosed; fords at which these troops would hesitate; steep cliffs from which they would fall whinnying or mooing; embankments that would slow them down; caves in which they would confine themselves to give birth, survive, hibernate, claw the walls. Technique is the end without end of human societies.

The *approche*—approach—is purely offensive; it is solitary, it is heroizing. It presupposes an extraordinary

PASCAL QUIGNARD

knowledge of the milieu, of the behaviour of the wild game, of its specific body, of its mortal anatomical spots. Thesis. The approach was the human hunt par excellence in pre-historic times. It defined how one became a hero in the most ancient societies. Having killed a bear all alone enabled the Inuit to call himself an inuit, that is, a man, that is, he who has survived a duel with the Erstwhile, with the old originary man (the cave bear) whose death dubs him, whose spoils consecrate him. A man is he who has killed his father and devoured him. The approach is the egalitarian con-frontation which gives the same fierce chances to the two animals facing each other. This hand-to-hand combat is the source of the duel of honour among the samurai of ancient Japan, at least until the imperial edict. This same combat formed the strange initiation rite of French nobility, among aristocrats, under Louis XIII, at least until the royal edict.

*

Five specific kinds of knowledge derive from the five hunting strategies brought to light by pre-human societies. These five kinds of knowledge 1. brought to life the milieu (separated *être* [beingness] from *l'étant* [that which is]), 2. made otherness surge forth in sameness (invented the intra-specific enemy), 3. qualified death and reproduction (by joining them in linguistic nomination), 4. agglomerated societies against the third party considered to be hostile (initiated the State in opposition to solitude).

Human society, structured in great genealogical strips, then subdivided into geographical cities, is only one of the five kinds of knowledge.

Scholium. *Society constitutes only a fifth of the originary science.*

*

Plato wrote in Protagoras 322a: At the origin, human beings lived in a scattered way (sporades).

*

Can one who is famished, one who is thirsty, one who is desirous—the solitary stalking undertaken by one who hunts, the tension (orexis) of one who thinks, research become purely intellectual—escape from the hallucinated predation that anticipates real predation? Never. Can this hallucinatory character emancipate itself from dream? Never.

This is how the noetic is forever devoted to what is absent by means of the olfactive. Then to what is absent by means of the oneiric. Then to what is absent by means of the linguistic.

Odour comes on behalf of flesh. The image comes on behalf of the silhouette (then the letter takes the place of the silhouette following upon the demi-rotation of the unreal originary line). Sound comes on behalf of the thing.

※

Can intellectual research hope to slip away from the collectivity which eats what it hunts, which reproduces its language by presupposing it in each little child that its members reproduce during copulations that conceive them following upon the deaths that select them and, one by one, relay their names to them? Can the noetic become conscious? Lucid? Rhetorical? Literal? Literary? Can the noetic nurture the illusion to one day differentiate itself from the mythic? Can it detach itself from the narrative whose subject is the *socius* (the reproduction of the herd in the depths of oneself)? Can it leave religion (the destruction of wild animals in nature) or tragedy (the destruction of heroes in history) or the police novel (the destruction of criminals in the city)? Can it make the famous first-person plural used by philosophers—which asserts the truth of *their* pack— implode at its source? Can it break free of group pressure until it becomes speculative?

※

Can what has been re-bound be unbound?

*

Research that becomes conscious of its functioning discovers that it has no purpose. It is a quest. It is pure savagery: solus vagusque. The word 'savage', which can be decomposed into the two short Latin adjectives 'solus' and 'vagus', names he who wanders alone in the forest. He who 'wanders alone' in the saltus or in the covert is the hero of the approach. Inside him, the pack distances itself. Inside him, the first realm is the nearest one or, at least, the realm that is the least forgotten one possible. Inside him, servitude ceases to be voluntary. It is the opposite of a destiny, that is, of a sideration: it is a de-orbiting. A 'solitary wandering' in time, in the milieu, in space, in what is possible.

*

If the noetic unbinds Ariadne's thread with respect to the signified world, that is, with respect to the mythic world, then it is a rhetoric.

If the noetic unbinds Ariadne's thread with respect to the ontogenetic metamorphosis during the acquisition of the group language, then it is an analytic.

If it manages to unknot the knot of Ariadne's skein and suspects a 'bondless' situation with respect to the signified, an empty place in the depths of everything, then it is an aporetic.

I had first titled this volume *Fundamental Noetics* to win back the soul to that which founds the double world. (To win back the soul, not only to that which founds it, but to that which founds.) To the bond of inclusion itself, which is only a bond to the Lost. To win back the soul to the bond, of the Lost, to the void. To the old cord that led all the way to her, the Lost. To the 'thread'. It is a matter of re-finding the thread of one's thought, from void to void, in order to be able to deploy, suddenly, at every station of the wandering, the possibility of a genuine *speculative rhetoric*. Therefore, *Fundamental Noetics* founded *Speculative Rhetoric*. Therefore, the initiate joined the sanctuary of the goddess Aditi.

*

The basis of the noetic quest is perhaps this: it is a matter of recuperating the lost fields of psychism which have been won from the enemy. It is a matter of winning over some post-language from the pre-language and from the human interdependence of which it is the vector. Thesis. The definition of mythic thought is simple: If myth is the narrative that founds the group, then inside this narrative (the transmitted language) the narrator is the group that commits its five hunting strategies to the milieu that it gradually distinguishes in the ambient domination. The pack remains the master, however little synchronized it is to the new times.

If thinking depends on the collective language acquired in the ancestral language of the group, can thinking unthink, dis-pense with, dependence? No. No group has 'invented' the language that it speaks. No subject has experienced the past that he relays. The palpitation in any-one's heart is not triggered by the heart—but by the pulse of one's mother's heart. The language is not itself invented by the groups that speak it. In an odd way, its nature is by no means artificial or technical. (It is neither divine nor human, but it is without a nomothete and it is nonthetic.) The magnificent theoretical possibility that Étienne de La Boétie outlined is impossible. One can liberate oneself as much as possible but one cannot be free. If thinking depends on the collective language acquired in the natural language, can thinking think, as much as possible, its dependence as that which is anterior to the group that has solidarized the language? Perhaps a little, indeed. One can even die for thinking.

*

This is why one must contemplate the void before anything else. One can be reborn from dying. (One can be thrown off one's saddle, baffled.) One can die of thinking. (Thought has content.) Birth can be pursued in its strange wandering fright. (One can be reborn. One can recommence one's life.) The first world can put forward its snout into the second world. The first realm still reigns over the last realm. The erstwhile still surges forth. The sun still shines. That which is most ancient in time is bound to that which is most spontaneous in its form.

Scholium. In this, nature is the best of that which is visible.

Its gushing forth still gushes forth from *behind* the primal visibility. Nature is still a strange retrospective glance. In German, this is the word Rückblick. In Greek, the word is hypsi. Latin appeals to the sublime. It is the highest part of the mountain before dawn.

Even as the dizziest and steepest thing is the sheer cliff.

Even as the most extravasated summit of a volcano is where the heart of the earth emerges, where its fire, its iron, its lava, its smell of sulphur, its pulsation of light overbrim.

There, on the lips of which gathered together the first thinkers of the physis—from Turkey, from Greater Greece, from Sicily—until they leapt into it.

There, on the shores of which, thought premeditates the hunt and the return from the hunt, the hearth, the return from fishing, the port, which is anticipated in what is dreamt, which advances in *narrative forms*, which is accomplished in linguistic lying, continues to play with ante-history.

In *novels*, the old predation re-immerges inside groups of images.

In *essays*, the old predation gradually emerges from reused codes; it surfaces above past experiences, ruins, 'museumified' human works, vestiges of sites, clouds, traumatisms, floods before History.

As the *feed-back* of what has been abandoned, as the reorganization elsewhere, this arrangement after the dis-arrangement is rather similar to the functioning of dreams. It prepares the second joy which advances in the metaphor, in the local relocation, in the transfer of identities, in an attempt at rewilding which manages more or less to make the junction with the savagery of the origin. The boomerang function relays the enantiodromia of consciousness. The second joy entirely consists of the pleasure of lifted inhibition. What impeded comprehension *spins* off at top speed, unwinds as if by miracle, sometimes suddenly dissolves in a fluidity that has never been seen. Like, on a mountain slope, a torrent ripping up its water on the rocks.

Every one, in the written language, crumbles bit by bit in a few seconds. Suddenly de-mosaics. It is like mist lifting over a Latin landscape—on the bluish hills of Latium, of old Etruria—at daybreak, progressively as the white star covered with mist which is born of its own warmth rises in the sky. It is knowledge of the third kind, according to Baruch Spinoza. According to him, it is laetitia accompanying claritas. A kind of inner sun more ancient than the outer sun begins to irradiate the ensemble of forms which, in fact, are but enigmas. A kind of tonic, a harmonic chord, begins to jingle along the entire thread of the first line (la prima linea) that the human being's way of looking invents on the horizon of his or her sojourn at the other end of his or her vision. Along the entire front in war. Along all the 'panoramy' of the milieu from the lookout over the site. Along all the skin or fur of the animal body in a sexual embrace. It is the jubilatio, the non-oblivion, the a-letheia of the truth, the ev-angile (go-spel), the good news that burns one's lips (and that one is dying to know) and sharpens one's claws. And every one who hears the news wants to give the alert for this piece of news that sets his or her body on fire. It is like this dawn that itself *provokes* the song or chant that *hails* it to the extent that one no longer knows what awakens, be it the light that pierces the edge of the horizon, or the beak that half-opens, or the flower that spreads out its petals. In thought, something mysteriously sounds the victory in a dawn relay. The new hypothesis is in the process of redistributing the whole field. Eureka is the cry made by Archimedes when he wants to share his discovery with the whole group; he is naked; he is in the bathtub; he forgets that he is naked; he runs down the streets of Syracuse set on fire by the Romans of Marcellus. Dripping wet, he shouts: Eureka. This cry that he makes is an aorist. It is the verbal tense of afterwards. I have found. He dies. It doesn't matter that he dies. It doesn't matter that the world is in flames. It doesn't matter that the naked, ash-covered butoh dancer now crawls through the ruins of Hiroshima Port in the August sun. The aorist has regained the present as its explosive core while we—all human beings, dogs of human beings, seagulls of human beings, swallows of human beings, around the point of impact or of projected shadow—moan, gasp, flee through the flaming port, flutter, are burnt to a crisp in the flaming port.

CHAPTER 17

On the Greek Crisis

Why was philosophy the dead-end specific to mythic thought in the West? Why did mythic thought, in a way that was as unpredictable as it was sumptuous, seek to de-mythologize itself in the western part of the world? It was an unpredictable moment in the fifth century BCE, at the border of the eastern world, during the non-intimidated rise to power of the gymnosophists of India and of the sophists of the East who travelled from caravans to caravans, from crossroads to crossroads, from fairs to fairs, from ships to ships, from ports to ports, in the ancient world.

The first philosophy was not first. Philosophy was a *reaction* to this wild wandering, of shamanic origin, which spread from Lake Baikal, which crossed the Bering Strait, which was gradually carried out in Asia and in Europe during the Neolithic period.

Philosophy indeed meant to be an anti-sophistry. To the free play of language, from the hallucination of what is dreamt, Buddhism responded by the disintegration of this hallucination (in Sanskrit, nirvana), and philosophy responded by truth (in Greek, aletheia).

The word nirvana means extinction. To extinguish the reflection. The word a-letheia means non-oblivion. To not forget, behind the silhouettes projected on the opposite wall, the light that illumines them. The philosopher refuses to snuff out the wick. To Middle-Eastern ascesis, the philosophy of the ancient Greeks responded by a *paideia* assigning its end inside the polis. To noesis, philo-sophia preferred the pedagogy of little children and put forward the political constitution of autonomous cities, each of them jealous of their hegemony. Education initiates one to constituted knowledge, moors itself to the deliberation of the assembly, gulps down the psychic world into political fascination, the orientation of virtues, the hierarchy of values, the constraint of laws, the fear of judges. This community integration is its particular joy. Its task is to thoroughly subjugate the subject. It is the happiness of belonging. It is the politeia.

However, this inclusive faculty is contrary to wandering thought (to the aporetic quest), even as *savoir*—knowledge—is the opposite of *connaissance*—becoming acquainted with. Knowing and becoming acquainted with are heterogeneous. The shaman was rejected to the margins of the hunting group (adolescent and adult males, all carrying spears) and excluded from the hearth (at once feminine, infantile and senile).

The secession of spirit hunters and their solitary life began long before History, long before the politization of Greek cities, long before the mythification of the great narratives. Even long before the first cities of the Neolithic world. Thought began long before Athens, Rome, Alexandria, Byzantium, Bologna, Paris, Oxford, Berlin, Vienna. It began with the palaeolithic world, in the movement of approach that entrusts the hunter with a solitary exploit. The movement that presides over anachoresis is originary. It precedes Buddha himself. It is already in naked Shiva, ithyphallic and covered with horns in the pine forest.

*

Society and thought are heterotelic.

The ends of fascination and lucidity are opposed.

Knowing and becoming acquainted with do not want the same thing in the soul of human beings. Whoever thinks, betrays. His or her curiosity de-solidarizes itself with the other members of the group. And what surges forth as the content of his or her thought can be radically asocial. Each noeme is unpredictable to the noesis. In noetic activity, 'idem ipse rumpit' (that which is the same breaks itself). The subject becomes de-subjection. A disorienting transport. A transfer so effervescent that it goes all the way to the proposition of metempsychosis. Even as the neuronal mass is without an assigned preliminary end, and endlessly exploitable, the noetic trance is without an assigned preliminary end, an infinite dance.

The preference of the polis *usque ad mortem*—such was, on the contrary, the philosophical preference.

Its martyr was Socrates.

The Greek word paidagogia (pedagogy) refers to a slave who leads a child from one point to another in the city of his fathers. Pedagogical indicates the servile activity that accompanies the little child to lead him from a (linguistic) code to a (political) norm.

A silence—an *en-fance* (infans, childhood)—is thus led to war by language.

*

To what extent can a political subject (a citizen) play with the language that he must reproduce in its codified graphism and in a blind reflex of obedience to the laws of its grammar?

To what extent can noetic exertion dis-enslave one from the subjugation of guilt, from the gaze of the family, from the viewpoint of the city, from the jealous distrust of the State, from the surveillance of morality, education, knowledge, law?

At the end of the Neolithic period, in the East, such is Zhuang Zhou, in China, leaving the city, refusing to give counsel to the prince, returning to the forest. Such is Heraclitus, in Turkey, leaving Ephesus, refusing to be king, climbing the mountain, dying under the stones thrown by children.

*

To what extent, in our time, in European societies, isn't psychoanalysis still a Greek philosopher who sets forth a destiny of integration? To what extent isn't the psychoanalyst still a pedagogue? He who leads a puer in the opposite direction towards the infans? He who makes language re-espouse its learning process? No—in that beyond anamnesis, analysis leads to the originary mystagogy that philosophy has forgotten: an initiation into the mysteries of the sky, of life, of nature, of dreaming, of desire, of sexuality, of the night.

Here is the old Taoist shaman once again. He emerges from behind that strange face. He trembles behind that strange bowtie.

Thesis. The fundament of analysis was to tear the great secret from the viviparous night. The year is 1899. It is possible that psychoanalysis reacclimatizes language to its originary conditions. It is possible that it manages to replunge language into its ante-linguistic, arbitrary game of images. I experienced it as a reintroduction into the animal world and its sequences of spontaneous hallucinations. It demythologizes the familial network. It de-subjects the political 'subject' from focal, familial, urban, social, national and warring interdependence.

✻

Sophistry, rhetoric, psychoanalysis, the silent (premeditated, individualized) inscribing of the letters of literature do not neglect the cause that is more ancient than they are, which is the savage force (alke) that inhabits language itself to the extent that it draws on it.

Contrary to rhetoric, philosophy forgets the medium. Philosophy withdraws its hand from the wall—at the spot where the literary person's hand is engulfed, where his eyes approach, where his soul listens.

✻

But the old Palaeolithic text can still be read beneath the new kind of writing that revolutionized a few languages spoken in the eastern part of this world, during the Neolithic period. The Greeks of the Asian coasts, at the end of the eighth century, by metamorphosing the old narration, transformed the *genre*. They transformed myth into dialogue. A para-sophy was called philo-sophy. A post-tyranny, because of the special use that it made of slavery, was called in Greek demo-kratia (power left to the people), in Latin res publica (a thing belonging to all placed in the eyes of all). Dialectics and the oratory art were the heart of this; the assembly of free men (the boule, the senate) was the end. However, whatever their 'community' will was, the philo-sophos did not entirely leave the sophos. The philosopher remained under the regime of the shaman, the magician with a voice and voyages. It was not thought that was called into question in the condemnation that the Athenians brought down on Socrates by a majority of 281 votes: it was the belief in this demon that the thinker did not intend to renounce.

CHAPTER 18

Apuleius on the Road to Alexandria

The emperor Titus Antoninus was reigning back then. As Apuleius was journeying to Alexandria, at the very moment he entered the suburbs of Oea, he fell off his mule onto the stones of the path. His ankle was wounded. He tried to stand back up, but the pain was wrenching. He again attempted to stand on his two legs but he fell a second time. He tried a third time, suffered a third time, and fell back again. So Apuleius the Dancer remained on the ground, sitting among the rocks. Two fishermen discovered him immobile, unable to use his legs, on the dusty path. They carried him in their arms inside the nearest villa. This villa belonged to Pudentilla. Pudentilla was a patrician, a widow, the mother of young Pontianus and of the much younger Pudens. She brushed a balm over the foot of the philosopher-orator and bandaged it. She gave him lodgings in one of the most beautiful rooms of the villa. This room had a terrace overlooking the sea. Apuleius liked it there. He stayed. They spoke. They loved each other. He wrote. This is how Pudentilla married Apuleius.

However, Pudentilla's son Pontianus rebelled against the remarriage of his mother.

In 158, Sicinius Emilianus, the brother of Pudentilla's first husband, took advantage of the African tour of the proconsul Claudius Maximus to accuse Apuleius of witchcraft as well as illegal appropriation of inheritance to the detriment of his nephew Sicinius Pudens. The lawyer Tannonius drafted the indictment. He intended to prove that the 'philosopher' was in fact a mage (magus) who had cast a spell on Pudentilla's mind and body. Slaves testified that they had seen Apuleius worshipping obscene statuettes dissimulated under a handkerchief (sudariolum). They added that he loved looking for a long time at his reflection in mirrors and that he made speeches to it. They swore that he hypnotized children by magic and diverted them from the virtuous path.

The trial took place in 158, in Sabrata.

Apuleius wrote his *Apologia* to justify himself.

Claudius Maximus managed to clear Apuleius of the charges.

Apuleius was declared 'non magus'.

But the arrest and the trial transformed Apuleius' life. He abandoned philosophy for the novel. He composed the admirable *Metamorphoses*, called *The Golden Ass* in our day, which is the story of a man who, nurturing the desire to transform himself into an owl in an olive grove, becomes a donkey wandering along the coast of Africa in search of a rose garden. He left Oea. He wanted to go back to the places of his childhood and adolescence. He moved. He left with Pudentilla for Carthage. With Pudentilla, he had a son whom they called Faustinus. This first witchcraft trial, at the beginning of Roman Antiquity, instituted by Sicinius Emilianus, pleaded by Tannonius and judged by Claudius Maximus, the proconsul of Africa, marked the origin of the Western legend of Faust.

CHAPTER 19

Socrates' Death in Athens

He was usurious, talkative, importunate, ugly, married, the father of three boys, a native of Alopeke. His parents were truly poor. His father was a sculptor's assistant. His mother earned her livelihood as a midwife. As an adolescent, he was fascinated by the speeches of the sophists, the glory that they enjoyed, the wealth that they amassed. During the battle campaign of Potidaea, he experienced an ecstasy. He remained standing, for 24 hours, from sunrise through the next sunrise, facing the sun. He desired to develop a way of confronting speeches (logoi) in order to 'turn' them towards the sun of truth (aletheia). At Delphi, Apollo asked him to devote himself to this 'turning' while he was in the god's sanctuary. Back in Athens, Socrates experimented with this new method of confronting the logos. On the one hand, in the streets, in the shops, in the gymnasium, in the gardens, on the docks, on the riverbanks. On the other hand, in the 'dialogos' that the soul carries on with the mysterious voice that it discovers inside its body, by which men and women can speak to themselves: the vocalization of the acquired language that becomes like a private god in them who speaks all by itself.

Tirelessly questioning everyone, he aroused the animosity of most of the adult citizens. He fascinated the youngest ones to the extent that they followed him everywhere in his quest and were won over by his fervour. He called into question all the kinds of logos: proverbs, moral maxims, kitchen recipes, deductions made by physicists, ancient customs, craftsmen's adages, paternal authority, civic laws, the gods of poets.

It happened that a rich tanner, whose name was Anytos, had a son who followed with a special fervour the teachings that Socrates gave in the streets. Anytos was a genuine democrat. He had been proscribed to Phyle. He had taken part in the overthrow of the Thirty Tyrants. Anytus went to find the tragic poet Meletus the Poet. They both joined the orator Lycon. It was Meletus the Poet who submitted the complaint to the registry of the archon-king, accusing Socrates not only of lacking piety with respect to the gods that the city venerated atop the hill, but also of introducing new gods in the form of secret, intermittent, non-visible voices due to the presence, in the soul, of a demon of an unknown nature.

In the year ~399, in Athens, 557 years before the accusation of witchcraft brought against Apuleius in Sabrata, an accusation of the capital crime of impiety was levied against Sokrates of Alopeke, son of Sophroniscus, which resulted in his death. At the time, Socrates was 70 years old.

Meletus' indictment uses the word theos to name the traditional gods and the word daimon to refer to the surreptitious voices (daimonian kaina, new demons) among whom the people of Athens included Socrates' god.

The tribunal drew lots for 502 citizens of more than 30 years of age. The tragic poet spoke first, the tanner second, the orator at the end. Socrates said nothing. He was sentenced to death, in a democratic way, by a clear majority of 281 votes. Why didn't Socrates defend himself? When Hermogenes, the son of Hipponikos, informed him that he needed to prepare his defence, Socrates responded that he had of course thought about preparing his 'apologia', but that his 'daimon'—this new god that the indictment accused him of introducing into the souls of young citizens of the city of Athens—had told him not to do anything. Socrates was led from the tribunal to the prison so that he would drink the hemlock. So he drank the cup, lay down on his back, showing his face, asked Kriton to sacrifice a cock for Asklepios. The coldness rose along his stomach. He had a short convulsion and his daimon went off to Hades.

CHAPTER 20

Biography and History

There is no Ancient Greek word for 'consciousness'. And even if two Greek words are brought together, nor did the word 'biography' exist among the Ancients. The form 'biographia' appeared for the first time in the text that the great Platonist metaphysician Damaskios the Diadoxos devoted in 530 (that is, 929 years after Socrates' death) at King Khosro's court to his master, Isidore, during the period in which the philosopher, having been persecuted by the alarming Christian sect which had closed the doors of the Academy, had had to flee Athens for Persia.

This was a time when Persia, in the holy war that the Christians were waging against the entire earth, was a Holland.

It was not 'biography' but 'History' that took the Greeks by surprise in the fifth century before the Christian era. They developed this strange enquiry (historia) regarding the past. But consciousness, the 'new demon', the human psyche revealing itself to be partly autonomous, left them speechless.

What is a Greek 'subject'? A way of acting in the city, nothing about private life hidden from sight, nothing about reproduction or childhood, both derived from animality or chance, both nestled in the gynaeceum, possibly one or two heroic memories of the war waged against the barbarian army that threatens to invade, or against the rival city that one wants to weaken, some memorable replies pronounced at a ripe age against tyrants, finally, if possible, a sublime word uttered at the moment of breathing out one's last breath (psyche) in front of everyone.

In no case is there an anchoritic innerness (a conscious-ness) in Ovid as exile, remorse, the withdrawal into language, the anxiety of unbelief and the relegation prolonged until death began to do their work in him in his two sad books, twice sad and so melancholy, which belong to the last years of his life, at the very beginning of the Christian era, on the shores of the Danube.

But even the *Tristia*, at the beginning of the Empire, do not yet constitute a dialogue with oneself such as Augustine develops it with genuine genius, with a sudden and extraordinary ampleness, in the books of his *Soliloquies*, then in those of the *Confessions*, in the last years of the fourth century.

Oddly, the Greek who, when dying, asserted a personal demon (an inner voice that inhibits action or that represses desire) found no 'biographer'. That his example did not contribute to the invention of that literary genre whose birth might have coincided with that of history. Neither Plato nor Xenophon wrote the life of Socrates, expanded upon his life's journey, detailed or explicated the chronicle of the rather mysterious demonry for which he died. They limited themselves to gathering public acts and wise words that marked the life of the city, to which they adjoined two apologetic fictions whose nature is, in each case, so puzzling that they have remained in our culture with the fabricated titles *The Apologia of Socrates* and *Memorabilia*. The *Apologia* of Socrates is a fake because he refused, in ~399, to make this apology in front of the tribunal of the Athenians. *Memorabilia* is a more inexplicable missense. I don't know why Xenophon's *Apomnemoneumata* is translated as *Memorabilia* and Epicetus' *Apomnemoneumata* by *Interviews*. In both cases, *Apomnemoneumata* means 'Memories'.

The Romans more soberly preferred to translate the word *Apomnemoneumata* into Latin as *Commentarii*.

Xenophon and Plato never dreamt of recounting the life of a man whom they had followed for years in the streets. Nor was the majority of the free citizens who reigned over the disproportionate mass of slaves in Athens curious about the destiny that this man had known before they decided to put him to death by 281 votes (against 221 citizens who preferred that he continue to live in the company of his demon while pursuing his inquiry in the streets of the city—or, rather, big village—sheltered by its majestic hill covered with olive trees and populated by owls).

Xenophon and Plato preferred to pursue the strange exploration which he had begun and in which his martyrized phantom held down the role, beyond his personal death, at once of a guardian and a guide.

Socrates became the angel who protected Plato in the unexplored areas of inquiry that he had himself tested in the shops of tradesmen, in the stalls of craftsmen, in the port of Piraeus, on the shore of the Ilissos.

This is how Sokrates became the great Daimon that presided over the religious journey which Aristokles, nicknamed Plato, resolved to call 'philosophia' and whose specific ascesis he himself radicalized.

*

Because the Romans were unaware of the institution of the gynaeceum, because they were subjected to a less liturgical religion whose gods were above all ancestors, because they conserved their specific faces, after having made their impression in wax, in a small private cabinet inside their

houses in the atrium, as opposed to the Greeks and before
the Christians, they had a passion for all the possibilities of
veristically representing private life: busts, paintings,
collections of antiquities, *apomnemoneumata* which
became *commentarii*, isolated anecdotes, lists of gossipy
items about indecent, sexual quirks. *Ragots*, pieces of
malicious gossip—such is the name of the young boars that
scavenge through garbage. Biography, like novel writing,
derived in Rome from the rite of the saturae, themselves
linked to the 'ludibrium', that is, to the sarcastic potpourris
of funerals. Biography is by no means related, in its
European origin, to the chronology of a journey of living
beings or heroes on the earth or on the sea. Biography is
linked to a realistic imprint, as Romans would begin their
mourning by detailing the features of corpses in bee wax:
an imago of the ancestor with his warts and his familiar,
vulgar, or sordid expressions, an imago made as much as
for touching as for laughing. Even Jesus' death is a
ludibrium. A crown made of opposing thorns that make the
forehead bleed instead of honouring it, a false purple cloak
resulting from whip straps, a sceptre deriding a royalty that
reigns over nothing.

*

Apuleius is a genius. Better still: he is the genius of genius. He is the author of one of the four universal masterpieces in the obscene, barely-anthropomorphic genre of the novel. Apuleius' life passion was curiositas, an already medieval, already encyclopaedic curiositas. He claimed that nothing was impossible, in his eyes and to his willpower. In Latin: Ego nihil impossibile arbitror. The subject of the 11 books of Apuleius' *Metamorphoses* is this: a man transformed by desire into an animal wants to become human again.

To put this in Greek: a theriomorphosis, which is the destiny of everyone, is followed by an interminable anthropomorphosis which does not succeed.

There are two worlds that can never be exchanged. The two realms of the experience of men and women.

It is the task or the illusion of our life to attempt to go from one to the other.

Apuleius slipped the tale of Psyche and Eros into the heart of this novel. The psyche hears a 'certain bodiless voice'. The psyche then holds out an oil lamp to surprise the body of the wild animal that has subjected her—the strange 'monster' of her desire. The soul holds out the light to her own night, and a drop of burning oil falls on the daimon's naked shoulder. This drop is transformed into a wing. The daimon Eros, become a bird, alights just as soon on a cypress branch in front of the window of the room where the soul had fallen asleep.

Who can see the erect sexual organ at one's own source?

Who is the woman and who is the man who can incur the ordeal of rebecoming an animal and holding out the light farther than oneself in time, at the heart of night?

*

The speech titled *De deo Socratis* was written by Apuleius before the *Metamorphoses* or *The Golden Ass*. It was pronounced by Apuleius at Sabrata, then at Carthage, to which he habitually rode astride a donkey or a mule, going along the Lake of Tunis.

This unique testimony about the 'god' specific to Socrates is invaluable and yet the words used by Apuleius exhibit a disconcerting status.

They lead astray.

In the eyes of both the Greeks and the Romans, two classes of animate beings were opposed: those that never die and those that die. The abyss separating the two kinds of animals was uncrossable: this abyss was, in fact, death itself. Its expanse was that of the sky. The Greeks said:

Theos anthropo ou mignutai. Mortals and immortals are immiscible. The Romans said: Nullus deus miscetur hominibus. No god descends among humans to get involved with the conditions of their sojourn. No communication went back up from passion to impassibility, from corruption to incorruptibility, from morality to immorality. The gods visible during the day (the sun, lightning), the gods visible at night (the moon, the stars), the invisible gods (the gods of Olympus who appeared to the inhabitants of our world only in forms borrowed from this world), ever since the time of the aedes, then ever since the time of the mythographers, keep distancing themselves ever more, from planet to planet, in the aether. Like the things in the words that indicate them, the gods faded away among the stars which, by associating themselves, composed their figures in the night sky. The Neolithic world burnt out. Just before the Christian world, in the eyes of the Stoics of Rome, the gods finally lost all contact with the human species, which addressed them with ever more abstract sacrifices.

The Epicureans had themselves contributed, in turn, to the pushing back of each of these two worlds to the extent of definitively making them refractory to each other.

This is how the gods found themselves locked up in the rarefied air, like Tiberius in desolate Capri.

Like a completely new total power—without compensating conditions—and a world government—without an opposing block—in the hands of an emperor himself devoted to the pacification of space, to the completely new obsequiousness of men in bondage, to apotheosis and to the celestial sidus.

Apuleius wished to re-establish the rainbow. A shamanic bridge led from the peaks to the mists. From the mists to the clouds. From the clouds to the stars. This is what Apuleius of Madauros asserts in *De deo Socratis*: There is an intermittent acquaintance and there is even an intermittent *contact* between things that are immiscible. Humans are not relegated to the earth as if to a kind of Tartarus. The air extends between the sky, inhabited by the immortal bodies of the gods, and the earth, sojourn of the bloody bodies of men and women who are still alive. The air also has its inhabitants, like the sky its divine animals, like the earth its mortal animals. Birds are not the genuine inhabitants of the air because they sleep and nest on the ground and because they are powerless to fly above the high mountains. This is why the Greek daimons, and the Roman genii, transformed themselves into animalia that were half-psychic, half-bird, halfway between the mortals and the immortals, halfway between mountains and the sky, in charge of occupying the interval separating them.

Apuleius, in the Roman soul, hung consciousness on the daimon by means of genius.

Apuleius was the last novelist to be accused of thaumaturgy. The last magus. In this sense, the cause of his defence in *Apologia* 28.3 and in *Florida* 10.3 is the same as that of *De deo Socratis*. They represent two remains, of prehistoric shamanism, which are deployed in the memory of a man who is dying in his cell, eating small hemlock carrot roots in order not to betray his demon and in the adventure of *Metamorphoses*, in which a man still roams, astride a horse, on the winds among the reigns and the worlds.

It is because the daimons occupy the interval of the air, between humans and gods, that they, therefore as superbirds, are provided with wings. On Etruscan, Roman, or Alexandrine frescoes, the two main demons, Cupido and Somnus, are always represented with enormous wings, white or yellow for desire, black or blue for sleep. What is this 'halfway' between earth and sky? It is the pale moon that marks the limit between the air and the sky. The moon is the angel that guards the sky. She is the genius of the genii because she is the mistress of the lunar blood shed by all women and whose absence signals the conception of the enfant in the depths of their abdomen, which is as invisible as it is dark. But if the moon is the last of the daimons, she is also the first of the theoi. In this sense, the moon is the god whose metamorphosis marks the time when one lifts one's eyes to the night sky. The almost-transparent demons fly to her and are moved: they moan and turn around her. Neither the stars of the true gods, nor living men and women, ever make their way into Hecate's company. Only demons approach Hecate, the queen of Hades (literally, in Greek, the origin of 'the Invisible'). Psyches are gradually purified in the sublunar air by dint of going in circles around the celestial body like transparent great cormorants. A few men, a few women, like the male and female shamans who would fall to the ground by whirling around themselves during the comings and goings that result from their trances, enter into communication with them, between the aether and the earth.

This is how one must comprehend Apulelius' statement, in his treatise *On Socrates' Demon*, that Socrates *saw* his daimon exactly as Achilles *saw* Minerva.

Neither Plato, nor Xenophon, nor Aristoxenus had asserted this gift of clairvoyance beyond vocal hallucination, even if they had recounted the long ecstasy that Socrates had experienced at Potidaea when he stood facing the sun.

Even Joan of Arc did not claim to have 'seen' with her eyes the 'voice' that spoke to her in the field of Domrémy, towards Vaucouleurs.

Maximus of Tyre specified this point, in Greek, in his *Dissertations*: The daimon is a psyche lacking a soma, celestial but also *pathetic* (a bodiless soul which flies in the air, but which acquires affects and becomes 'passionate' once it has fallen into the world of humans).

Plato wrote in Greek in his *Laws*: In the same way that it is not oxen which guard herds of oxen, nor goats which guard herds of goats, demons are the guardians of humans who are excessively emotive, that is, melancholy humans. For it is to humans that is reserved the fright that derives from death and the affects of the desire awakened by dreams. Only gods know indifferent joy.

This is how that the daimons of the Greeks, and the genii of the Romans, ensured the metaxu, the medietas, the coming and going between high and low, between immortals and the dead.

As exchanger gods, demons are also the guardian gods of the exchanges that they offer. Sleep is the greatest metamorphosis possible (once the body has sunk into its pouch of hallucinations). Desire is the most pathetic of metamorphoses during the inflation of the phallos of the Greeks, during the erection of the fascinus of the Romans. Reflexion is another disquieting metamorphosis (into the specular double with which Narcissus is confronted and which is neither an oneiric phantom nor an erotic phantasm). In

Plato's Greek, guardian is phylax, supervisor. In Latin, these phylakes are called custodes, or testes: they are witnesses. There are always two of them. These two witnesses (testes) refer to the two testicles specific to the genitality of the genius situated beneath the erect fascinus (or below the suddenly flaccid penis, once the social reproduction is consummated). This is how the 'genius' specific to the Romans modified Socrates' 'daimon'. It offered its personal guard, and its genesic protection, to the guardian 'angel' of the Christians.

CHAPTER 21

I am gradually approaching the thinker in the thought. Apuleius translated daimon into Latin as genius. But Sokrates and Apuleius, separated by eight centuries, although speaking of the same thing and both taking the risk, following upon a public trial, to die of that thing that they think, do not speak of the same thing.

In ~399, Socrates, 70 years old, had himself defined what he meant by the word *daimon*. This definition is found in Plato, *Apologia* 31d: 'It is something that began in childhood (ek paidos). It is a certain voice (phone tis) which, when it makes itself heard, never prescribes (protrepei) what I must do, but diverts (aprotrepei) me from what I was going to do.'

It is an inner voice that revokes a thought. A halt that disengages a project, that defuses a desire, that represses a wish. It is a kind of inner whispering that diverts from action.

Plato procures another definition, which is not contradictory, but which leaves the psyche in a 'mysterious' silence.

In Greek: The demon (daimon) can take shape in a sign (semeion) that suspends without speaking. It takes on the appearance of a negation or an erasure that immediately cancels that which was elaborated in the mind. It is embodied in a strange 'stop' signal that leaves the soul without words.

*

Genius is the engendering god of the Romans. He is the god that renews bodies in the Empire. The ancient Romans lived under the protection of genii to whom they sacrificed sexual organs, the most beautiful sexual organs found in this world: flowers. A genius is he who engenders (gignit). The Romans said: Any man is a genius because my genius is that which engenders me. Genius meus nominator quia me genuit. This first guardian angel is a sexual conjurer angel. Genius is the god who protects the 'genitalia' of the Fathers. In the same way, the Romans called the double marriage bed the 'lectus genialis'. The 'genial' bed of the Romans is what the Italians today call the 'matrimonial' bed. If Fascinus is the god of the stiff virile sexual organ, he is still more precisely the god of the fascinatio which protects the male member from impotence or from flaccidity thanks to his statuette: the fascinum protector (which protects from impotence the male sexual organ for which it is the substitute). Like Socrates' semeion, the sign sculpted or modelled on the phallos (in Latin, the fascinum) is apotropaic; it prescribes nothing; it also retains. It silently *diverts* (aprotrepei) on the marble, or the bronze, or the leather, or the ivory, the desire of other men. It takes onto itself the fiascos of the flesh mentulae. It preserves the metamorphoses (mutationes) of the reproducers, for although it reproduces the family, the city and the Empire, the fascinus does not reproduce them each time unless it is erect.

*

Even as the celestial abyss between the immortals and those who die is uncrossable, the individual abyss (between oneself and its source) is also uncrossable.

No one can be present at the scene that engenders him, nor at the prerequisite erection, nor at the posture required by the sexual embrace. In Latin: an unknown imago stands like a guardian at the door of the individuum. This is why one cannot distinguish between the fascinating scene and the genial scene. We are never born from ourselves. In the villa of Mysteries, at a few kilometres from the ruins of Pompeii, after the wheat fields and the vineyards, in a basket of braided rushes, the fascinum is veiled with a dark handkerchief (like the object, under the linen sudarium, evoked by the prosecution against Apuleius).

This hidden god is the first of the daimons.

In other terms, he who engenders the daimons, Genius, is the lower name of Eros. It refers to the two 'testes' above which the fascinus erects. These testes are the Manes. Virgil writes in Latin in the sixth song of the *Aeneid*: Quisque suos patimur Manes. Each person undergoes his Manes. The Roman Manes are in the plural because there are two of them. The Manes are the two 'genii'—favourable and unfavourable, devoted either to potency or to impotency, pressive or depressive, dynamic or cowering—who fall to us at birth.

Philo the Jew wrote at the end of the first century: In cunctas animas in ipsa nativitate advenientes ingrediuntur duae simul virtutes, salutifera et damnifica. Into all souls, at the moment of birth, penetrate at the same time two virtues, one salutary, the other malevolent.

Even as genius translates the Greek daimon, virtus translates the Greek dynamis. In Old Roman, virtus always means violent virile sexual potency. Good demonry, the eudaimonia of the Greeks, becomes inflatio for the Romans. It is the auctoritas, that which grows. 'That which grows', literally 'augustus'—such is the nickname chosen by Octavian when he acceded to the Empire, before he himself gives his name to the fructifying month in the heart of summer. To comprehend the metamorphosis of daimon into genius, one must recall the first lines of the invocation to Venus which opens Lucretius' *De natura rerum*:

> Mother of Aeneas's sons, joy of men and gods, Venus the life-giver, who beneath the gliding stars of heaven fillest with life the sea that carries the ships and the land to Venus, that bears the crops; for thanks to thee every tribe of living things is conceived, and comes forth to look upon power of the light of the sun. Thou, goddess, thou dost turn to flight the winds and the clouds of heaven, thou at thy coming; for thee earth, the quaint artificer, puts forth her sweet-scented flowers; for thee the levels of ocean smile, and the sky, its anger past, gleams with spreading light. For when once the face of the spring day is revealed and the teeming breeze of the west wind is loosed from prison and blows strong, first the birds in high heaven herald thee, goddess, and thine approach, their hearts thrilled with thy might. Then the tame beasts grow wild and bound over the fat pastures, and swim the racing rivers; so surely enchained by thy charm each follows thee in hot desire whither thou goest before to lead him on. Yea, through seas and mountains and tearing

> rivers and the leafy haunts of birds and verdant
> plains thou dost strike fond love into the hearts of
> all, and makest them in hot desire to renew the
> stock of their races, each after his own kind. And
> since thou alone art pilot to the nature of things . . .

Immediately afterwards, one must read the invocation to the moon that closes Apuleius's novel. Lucius, the hero of animal metamorphoses, awakens on the beach of Cenchreae, in a state of sudden fear (pavore subito), as if he were being born. He sees the disk of the full moon emerge from the waves of the Aegean Sea. He stands up and runs towards the sea. He dips his head into the waves seven times. Then he invokes the queen of the sky (regina caeli) by using all the names that seem possible to him: Ceres, Venus, Phoebe, Proserpina, Diana, Juno, Hecate, Rhamnusia. . . . All these feminine figures come back at last into the soul of the hero who is being born. However, he who wanted to become a bird (and who has transformed himself into a donkey) is actually sleeping; his body is lying on the sand, on the shore of Cenchreae, his head between his hooves. The queen of the night, this time in the form of Isis, appears to him in a dream. She is crowned with a mirror. She is enveloped in the great black cloak of the night. This cloak is so densely black that she shines (palla nigerrima splendescens atro nitore). Isis then says to Lucius' daimon, who seems lifeless on the sandy shore while he sleeps: As the Mother of beings, the mistress of the elements, the origin and principle of the centuries, the supreme divinity, the queen of the Manes, the first and foremost among the inhabitants of the sky, the uniform mode of the gods and goddesses, I am Nature. I am the one who rules over the luminous vaults of the sky, the salutary breaths of the sea, the desolate silence of hell.

This is how the daimon of the nightly moon, that is, the goddess of the demons, the only influent goddess for the sublunar world, the guardian demon of the gods, suddenly became a substitute, in Ápuleius' world, for the solar Venus of Lucretius, of Caesar, of Augustus, founding the lineage of the Roman city ever since Anchises, legitimating the imperial genealogy and authorizing the divinization of the first emperors in the form of stars (sidera) that rise high in the sky and are inscribed in the firmament. In a first period, at the end of the Empire, Isis chased out Venus. In a second period, at the beginning of the Middle Ages, Yahweh chased out Isis. Christianism forced the demons to take refuge in the people of saints among whom, moreover, they multiplied in number, gradually dislodging the martyrs who had themselves taken the relay from the hero-hunters of wild animals. Even as Apuleius is the first Roman citizen of Antiquity to undergo a witchcraft trial, he is the first mage to draw up the genealogy and the hierarchy of the demons, the genii, the good genii, the guardian angels that Christianism had already begun to annex before dividing them even more in order to oppose them forever in the form of a daimon facing an angelos. Diabolizing the devil, making the god monotheistic.

CHAPTER 22

Pythagoras at Metapontum

In the Iatmul language, verbs signifying copulation are all transitive. Similarly in Greek: Logo sarx egeneto. The word became flesh. This word that has become flesh is God. The Latin translator (Saint Jerome) turns into the passive tense the most moving moment of the service: Et verbum caro factus est. Language was 'itself' made flesh in the little human one. And the Word being made into flesh—this is how language has come to inhabit the psyche of men and women, covering with a bloody sweat the faces of men in the fright of dying because of the resonance of the language introduced into them.

Pythagoras waited for the night, wrote the question preoccupying him in blood on a copper mirror, showed his face to the moon. Then the lunar reflection responded to the question that he had asked it.

This is how Pythagoras *read*.

One day, the same day, Pythagoras was seen in Metapontum and in Taurominium.

In the past, he had been Athalides, one of the Argonauts; he had been seen in ~1300, with an oar in his hands, sitting near Boutes, his swimming companion. He had been Euphoros, 400 years later, a soldier valorously fighting alongside Ulysses during the siege of Troy. He had been Hermotinos. Then Purrhos. Finally, he had been Pythagoras.

With the name of Pythagoras, he was the younger son of a ring engraver who lived on the island of Lemnos.

He went to Egypt, learnt the language, was taught the strange signs, and read them.

At last he settled in Italy in the city of Crotone. His daemon had preserved the memory of the circuit of his soul in different bodies. He had been wounded by Menelaus and suffered from this wound. With the name of Pyrrhos, he had been a Delian fisherman. With the name of Pythagoras, he had been the first man not to call himself a sophos but, out of modesty, or out of cunning, philosophos, that is, the assistant to the mage, he who accompanies the sophos, he who remains sitting next to him while the shaman's daimon leaves his body and journeys to who knows where in the three worlds.

CHAPTER 23

The Imaginary Companion of the Maternal Voice

Every survivor needs an imaginary companion. The imaginary companion is the voice that is more ancient than oneself. Every child has had a mother. This is how every thought has its Siren. In Greek, the word psyche means breath. How does the little newborn, abruptly won over to Breath by the cry that makes him palpitate as he leaves the first realm, recognize the lost body from which he comes? By hearing the voice of that body. Such is the psychic Ariadne's thread. The 'mother's voice' can become the 'mother tongue' 18 months later, because it was, for nine months, the soprano of the woman who bore the foetus and who enveloped it in her cadence and who inserted it into her song. In the new world, on the shore of light, it is her voice—its timbre, its intensity, its flow, its rhythm—by which the newborn recognizes its mother in the first immense 'object' that stands in front of him against the light, in her big dark cloak: a volume and a form which, until then, he had never seen and which bends down over him yet which speaks *in the same voice*, clearly more *ancient* than all the appearances. The only surviving object from the first world in which he lived buried, immersed, in the water of her pouch, is this voice that henceforth goes through the air to reach him. What bound the foetus to the gravid woman rebinds the newborn to the parturient woman, then the enfant to the mother. Ariadne's thread is this lost voice that comes back, this re-liaison which survives the extraordinary animal metamorphosis and which soothes its violence and suspends its traumatism. From this stems the indivisible bond between music and thought. The voice is that which leads from the uterine cavern to the cephalic cavern. Such is the siren who accompanies thought like a dog the hunter, like a falcon the knight, like a bull Pasiphae, like the moon the sun, like Ariadne Theseus.

CHAPTER 24

The Aphantos of the Word

In 65, under the emperor Nero, in the city of Antioch, Luke, a Greek doctor, began to transcribe a story pronounced in Aramaic and reported to him by Cleopas. This story is crucial if one wishes to meditate on the nature of thought. It dates to 464 years after the putting to death of Sokrates in Athens, to 93 years before Apuleius was accused of witchcraft at Sabrata. The first day of the week after the god was dead, at dawn, Maria of Magdala, Joanna and Maria Jacobi, the mother of James, as they were walking to the tomb where the body of Iesous had been placed, with spices in his hands, fire, ointments, balms, they found the stone rolled away, the unwound bandelettes at the back of the tomb.

No more body.

Suddenly the three women perceived two angels who were dressed in dazzling garments and standing on the edge of the tomb. The two angels said to the three women:

'What living thing are you searching for among the dead?'

*

The same day, two men who were disciples of this same dead Iesous (one of them being this Cleopas whose story Luke recounts) and who had left Jerusalem to go 60 stadia from there, to a village called Emmaus, saw a man—while they were conversing as they were walking down the road, while they were evoking the ignominious death of him whom they loved—quickening his pace and nearing them in order to take part in the discussion that they were having.

Cleopas was speaking of the sepulchre that had been found empty the same morning, of Maria of Magdala who had been emotionally overwhelmed, of the rolled-away stone, the unwound bandelettes at the back of the cavity of the tomb, the alarmed legionaries of Rome.

The three men kept walking along, Cleopas was talking.

When they arrived in Emmaus, night was falling.

And the mysterious man who had accompanied them up to now *pretended* to go further.

Et ipse se *finxit* longius ire.

Strange *fiction* by God who eternally feigns to say farewell in the 'Language' that he incarnates.

However, as soon as they perceived this movement of going off or even of fleeing, the two disciples urge the stranger to remain with them. They suggest that they have dinner together inside the inn. Cleopas says:

'Stay with us because the night is falling. Look! The day will soon be over.'

The stranger accepts. They enter the inn. The three men lie down on beds, rest on their elbows, wash their hands in the water presented to them.

The stranger took the bread. He broke it and gave it to them. And then, at the same time, their eyes opened, they recognized him, he disappeared in front of them.

Literally: He *vanished* in front of their *wide-open* eyes. Et *aperti* sunt *oculi eorum*, et cognoverunt eum, et ipse *evanuit ex oculis eorum*.

Luke's Greek is more precise and also transitive: He becomes 'invisible' (aphantos) in front of them.

He of whom you speak stands at your side.

Loving, desiring, sleeping, dreaming, or reading is this 'seeing the aphantos'.

Reading is to endlessly follow with one's eyes the invisible presence.

He whom your book evokes stands right next to your head. He or she is the being who stands closest to the side of your skull. Any being that stands in your thought has, with respect to you, more proximity than those closest to you can aspire to. And yet he or she of whom you think appears *thus,* in front of your wide-open eyes, *invisibly.*

The woman who is absent from every sexual embrace (that is, the woman of the embrace from which you proceed) follows you more closely than your shadow. It is said that she inscribes her features and desires over all the body. It is said that her phantom haunts the brain and wanders in the sublunar impassioned world to the extent of designating the chosen one or he who will look the most like him whom she loved.

He of whom you are reading the story is more you than you. He is nearer you than your hand that holds the book that your sight itself forgets while reading it. *Il est comme la prunelle de vos yeux*—He is like the apple of your eye. In Latin, *prunelle* is *pupilla,* the *petite poupée* (small doll). A little doll, because at the back of the pupil the tiny figure of the absent one is outlined. It is always the same wandering female demon.

The tiny figure of the invisible mother with whom all little girls play in real space.

He who passionately loves bends over the eyes of his beloved. He who bends over the eyes of his beloved discovers the minuscule miniature face of the desirous, lost young woman of whom he had been the invisible companion before dying in the first world to be reborn in the second world all alone, all naked, in the violent light, accompanied by a mere voice (psyche) indicating a source at which we no longer bathe our faces let alone our bodies while slowly swimming.

*

He who bends over the eyes of his beloved, with time, cannot be spared from terror. We must gaze very little into the depths of the eyes of him or her whom we love if we do not wish to find in them a face that has very little to do with personal facial features.

*

Orpheus flees Hades once he has perceived Eurydice's worm-eaten face. The worms were falling from her empty eyes. The worms were falling from her nostrils. The worms were falling from her half-opened mouth.

*

We must look very little into the eyes of the cats who nobly accompany our days. Otherwise, we would vanish from this world.

*

In the depths of every gaze reside importunate and beloved, terrified and terrifying demons.

They guard and they exchange.

*

Psychoanalysts call 'narcissistic guardian' the double who reassures an infant who contemplates himself in a mirror for the first time. This is also a fiction. Se finxit. He feigns to approach himself. He tries to approach 'self' of him. In this case, it is a daimon who allows one to approach one's personal reflexion. Ipse becomes idem. It must be admitted that a personal reflexion is the most pathetic reflexion that can fall into the eyes of men and women, and it is true that this first exchange requires at least one exchanger demon to watch over the implausible transaction to which a breath subjects itself when it falls nose-to-nose with both a rather specific face and a blatantly sexualized lower abdomen.

Novelists call 'imaginary companion' the beneficial double who keeps company with an infant alone in the darkness, or a mourning infant, or an abandoned infant, or an infant become who has become solitary.

The imaginary companion can be defined as 'he to whom the infant speaks while playing games.'

However, thought defines a game in which a being who is more or less unknown and lost is spoken to.

Whenever it pleases him, the infant summons up this invisible angel, speaks to him whenever he wants, dismisses him as he likes. He asks advice of him.

This demon, for an infant, as long as he doesn't speak, is not exactly hallucinated.

He is something both real and nearby, a twin, a beast with soft beastly fur, a playmate, a bit of silky odorous blanket at the end of his fingers, a bit of pillowcase at the edge of sleep, a thumb, a little finger, a guide and hero and sentinel, most often localized in the head or around the head, around the bangs of hair, around the nose and the mouth.

The old woman who speaks all alone also—she also still—turns her chin slightly to speak directly to him, the invisible one, in her mumbling.

CHAPTER 25

The Sylph

Men and women who touch their genitals while they are alone, having a nap, or at twilight, or also at dawn—either because the genius Cupido has unexpectedly visited them or because the genius Somnus has begun by erecting their body and then by guiding their hand to the nearest thing of themselves that is expanding and swelling—hallucinate a double that procures a more and more irresistible attraction to hardly voluntary scenarios in which they begin to take pleasure.

This double brings a non-negligible assistance to the pleasure which they expect from the end of their fingers.

*

We sometimes fall into an *inexpressible nostalgia* at the locus of these joys which would be shameful if we had to avow them to our loved ones during the day or to show them to our ancestors in the past. An exaggerated reverie is born and grows impatient. An imaginary sensuality grants the unavowable wish. A body that is not there comes to protect the overwhelming desire. It offers its guardianship to the idea that the soul rejects. It supports and it defends against the rising conscience. It survives the effusion. One falls asleep in its dream.

The angel guarding men and women during their forlorn joy, and making it blossom, is also a daimon.

A work by Crébillon, from 1730, is entirely devoted to masturbatory phantasms. Even as Socrates in ~399 had decided to call 'daimon' the inner voice, Crébillon decided to call 'sylph' this daimon of the solitary hand. Crébillon was 23 years old. 2,129 years had gone by since Socrates had died for his daimon, and Crébillon never pushed further on, in his subsequent works, the deep, inexorable boldness of this short volume. It is titled *Le Sylphe*. During his entire life, Claude Jolyot de Crébillon collected engravings. He moved to Sens, with Miss Stafford, in 1750, transporting more than 2,000 licentious images. This book ranks among the strangest and most astonishing books ever drafted about the life of human beings. It ranks among the best written in our language.

Why was Socrates stubborn to the point of defending this little repressive voice against everyone? Why did he give his life for this Tom-Thumb-like whispering? Why did he endure imprisonment, irons on his feet, then poison for something as problematical and invisible? Why did he remain faithful to this inner 'stop' to the point of not presenting his justification in front of the city, with the pretext that this 'voice' prohibited him from doing so? Why did Socrates show more courage and more resolution concerning these strange vetoes rising from the depths of his soul than Joan of Arc herself, threatened by the flames of the stake, who agreed to defend herself during her trial in Rouen?

Because this 'voice of the other' is truly stuffed into the mouth of every man and every woman.

Because this vocalization is as vital as the breath that is violently introduced into the body at birth.

It stands behind the language that it speaks.

The most ancient language, before becoming face-to-face discourse, is a visitation of voice. Language is an exchanger god as inner as outer, with prescriptions and interdictions, a rotation of yes and no, of authorizations and hindrances, of blessings or malefic modulations. It is, finally, a turnstile on which he or she who says *I* can wholly become *you*, on which the *you* who listens is already present in the *I* who expresses itself.

The egophoric exchange (the to and fro between *I*'s and *you*'s during an interhuman dialogue, which is always that of a maternal element and a filial one) is the demon of the demonic exchange and this is why the daimon prevented Socrates from responding at the tribunal, prevented him from accepting to detach the dialectic method from the demonic ecstasy, refused to disjoin the Pythia from the Rooster. In his *Lessons on the History of Philosophy*, Hegel is the only philosopher of the western tradition to have unreservedly faced up to the question of Socrates' cataleptic ecstasy at Potidaea. To have defined it as a tearing away of self from self. To have meditated on it as a 'secessus corporis' of thought and to have connected it to the romantic avowal of genius and to the invention of the dialogued method (in Greek: of dialectics). Hegel wrote: Socrates is the first man in whom what would later become a habit was manifested in a physical form. In 1836, F. Lélut followed this up: The Greeks transmitted this divinization of unwell thinking to posterity, as a heritage (*Du Démon de Socrate* [Paris: 1836], p. 149).

This divinization of unwell thinking is the first somatization of conscience. First of all, the convertibility of the listener into a locutor is the esoteric name of the anonymous demon. Secondly, dialectics is the theatrical mask (*persona*) that thought donned during the invention of philosophy in Athens.

*

In the first world, the inconvertibility is total.

On one side, in water, the content is a breathless listening; on the other side of the skin, the container is the child-bearer's solitary soprano voice.

The subject is presupposed in the son by the mother inside the language with which she addresses him.

*

In the second world, one can distinguish two cases of incontrovertibility between listener and locutor.

The first case is infancy. The infant is a listener who is, from birth, endowed with breathing but who is not yet a locutor of the national language. The infant is a hostage.

The infans (the non-speaker) is a hostage of the human language that the mother insinuates into him through her intonations and following the various orders with which she besieges him, or wraps him up, or constrains him, or strangles him. An 'infant' is a prisoner by violence of the voice which enjoins the movements of his body, whereas he proceeds from a world of shadow and silence, and which builds him as a subject in the maternal language in the eyes of everyone.

The second case is reading. Writing has its demon, as thinking has its demon—the same one. This is not the case of reading.

If literature is the ecstasy of language, reading, on the contrary, is the *return to the inconvertible language.*

A reader is not an in-fans, even if he does not speak. The reader is not a violated hostage, even if he is also a hostage. He is a hostage by consent to the violence that is going to be exerted on him by his reading of the other. He likes losing consciousness within this transfer to the state of freedom that is a novel. He likes to identify himself. A reader is this paradoxical trick: a former hostage by violence consents to subject himself once again to the first, inconvertible ordeal of a totally new, demonic, violent maternal language.

CHAPTER 27

De deo ignoto

The incessant discourse which, in each human being, formulates his life at the back of his or her skull is involuntary. In the conscious world, the Latin word 'conscientia' refers to this remaining strand of the Ariadne's thread of the sovereign woman's voice which tied together the two bodies and ensured a kind of coming-and-going between the two realms.

This constant, clandestine whispering which has roamed in the depths of the cephalic cavern ever since we attained the age of reason is less elaborated by us than we are constructed by it (that is, by that which escapes us during this tireless commentary that the acquired language sets off inside the cephalic cavern).

These are the strange apomnemoneumata or infinite commentarii behind the bone of the forehead, behind the eyes.

These spontaneous signs or inhibitions or preventive acts or prescriptions inside us, to which we are subjected as if they were orders (because, once we fail to obey them, they open doors of anguish inside us), following upon this rambling on from ourselves to ourselves, which we later call, indiscriminately, good conscience or bad faith, are more demonic than subjective, more demonic than 'personalizing', more familiar and social than individual or private.

Accepting not to be the father of one's thoughts was Socrates' first humility.

Socrates' second humility was that no discourse is in itself valid to direct itself towards the non-oblivion, but that only the conflict between at least two discourses can grope towards the true.

Actually, it is the same thing: demonic and dialectic both indicate that there exists no discourse that is uniquely and wholly one because language is not uniquely and wholly one. Through the dialogos by which the spoken language is learnt and through the double face of the linguistic system, through the 'manes' of the sexual conception of the non-speaking infant, we are bound to both the unknown and the lost. Everything which we say, which we don't know how to say or which we think we are saying, serves the unknown that beckons to us and that has sometimes remained, even more simply, the lost mother. It is this unknown which is inside us more than we are inside ourselves which Socrates began to call a demon. On Socrates' God means: Of the unknown God. *De deo Socratis* means *De deo ignoto*.

*

I don't know what I am doing. I don't clearly understand what I am in the process of writing. I hesitate in front of what I dream. I also know how not to know. An unknown demon speaks to me. Something sometimes stands above my shoulder. A sylph has taken up residence in my lower abdomen and near my scrotum and he holds out its images. I hear voices which have never existed and I note them down. Sometimes a drop of burning wax falls onto the fat of my right shoulder and the god flies off. I cannot give up these visitations which always leave me more alone and which distance me ever further from more savage, more ancient, more shadowy times. Two angels were standing at the edge of an empty sepulchre.

'Quid quaeritis viventem cum mortuis?' (What living thing are you searching for among the dead?)

'De deo ignoto.'

*

When a legionary informed Marcellus about Archimedes' death in a fire in the port and in the city, the Roman general wept. Why did Marcellus weep when he had himself given the order to set fire to Syracuse, knowing full well that the architect was present inside the city as tar-covered, flaming arrows were being shot onto the rooftops of the houses?

The officer persisted by asking his general-in-chief: What did he admire so much in this dead man whose name was Archimedes? His courage? His scorn for money? His virtue? His disdain of honours. His refusal to have power? His opposition to the Roman rule?

'Nothing of any of that', responded the general. 'I'm weeping over his muse. An endless passion brought him to science. It is the extraordinary *poiesis*, which urged him to develop techniques of all kinds, over which I'm weeping. You don't understand that *this man lived under the constant spell of a Siren who never left him and shared his life with him.*'

This is how Marcellus also wept over the Siren who had perished with Archimedes' soul in the fire of the city of Syracuse, which he was besieging.

*

In one of his most beautiful sermons, Meister Eckhart says that Mary Magdalene was horribly disappointed: When she expected to see Jesus, she saw two angels, when she expected one she saw two, when she expected Eternity she found Time, when she expected the former union she discovered language.

Why have men, why have women been led to bring back after life, alongside a Father himself officiating in the depths of the night of death, the unknown man who has engendered them after having denuded himself during a scene which they cannot have seen because they are the effect?

Why a unique Father after death? Because he was *inevitably unique* before the conception.

Magdalene, the saintly sinner, is disappointed because it is not a *unity* that rises in front of her body, in front of the pushed-back stone of the dead God. She is led back to the world of the living where there is no natural language that does not insinuate just as soon separation, interlocution, civil war into the body.

Homer's heroes still hysterically showed these Socratic dualities even if they did not take on the form of inner 'monologues'. They were always 'dialogues' that the aedes sang inside the hero's body. A hallucinogenic voice addressed the hero and long advised him by making speeches to him, by dialoguing with his heart, with his liver, with his breath, with his courage, like one man to another man. There are two unknown gods. There are two agnostoi theoi. There are two dei ignoti. There are two sexes which immediately differ like the Manes, that is, which immediately prescribe, at the moment of birth into the second life, the sexual difference as a tough, sempiternal destiny. One always dreams of it only as a single one—which is the other one.

*

An infant survives in the grip of the voice of she from whom he has come out through the sexual organ. As long as he will speak, as long as he will write, as long as he will think, he will be the hostage of the 'language of his mother'. Language is this leftover bit of goddess. She *is* this phantom of an angel capable of going from him to her and of coming back.

In the cradle, the cry is truly his angel.

The cry is the demon who goes from the infant to the mother, which brings her back to him.

All life long, for every book that one writes, for every temper that one raises, for every loving word that one pronounces, for every theory that one invents, language hallucinates a Lost One who comes back to take her place alongside the speaker. The hostage is the messenger's hidden face. Pater semper incertus. Mater semper certa. The mother is always certain, certissima, the father perpetually uncertain. This is why the saint is a prostitute and a sinner. In fact, there is no 'father', but the 'gignit', the 'he engenders', the erectio which stands alongside the engendered like a phantom, like an erstwhile, as his source. His destiny is that other sex which is his source—who holds his head against her hand, whose hair is undone, who stares at the candlewax burning down and god's skull.

*

Is the internalized tradition a guardian angel? Yes.

Is language a demon? Yes.

Are we as present in our dreams as our dreams are present in our lives? No.

Are we ourselves as present to ourselves as dreams are present in the genius that they contract, in the fascinus that they develop? Never.

*

Never has it appeared to me that we are much ourselves.

Never has it appeared to me even that we are as much ourselves as the demon who brushes up against us.

CHAPTER 28

The Invention of Conscience

At the beginning of the Christian era, in 12, in Tomes, Rumania, Ovid wrote: *Conscius* in culpa scelus esse sua. Conscious of being a criminal caught in his guilty act.

Conscience defines the guilt of the killing, be it an animal or a human death. We are afraid that the prey—which we devour each day—will turn against its predator, aspire to devour its devourer.

Paul writes in 57 to the Romans: Quod enim operor, non intelligo. Non enim quod volo, hoc ago. Sed quod odi malum, illud facio. Indeed, I do not understand what I do. Indeed, what I want to do, I do not do. But what I hate to do, I do. At this moment, in Paul's thought, the demoniac begins to become the diabolical. With Paul, it is no longer a matter of a voice inhibiting a bad act. It is the divine voice that is now hindered in Paul. And the linguistic voice no longer manages to hinder the unjust act from being committed. The soul begins to grow and to ask for more inside itself, to stand in opposition—as in a state of dialogue—to the body that it animates. The civil war (stasis) becomes inner, between the senses and the Word. Saint Paul writes: Another law fights against the law of my reason and holds me captive by the law of sin residing in the members of my body.

Lex mentis: it is less the law of reason (ratio) than the law of the functioning of thought (mens).

I like the definition of conscience given by Guibert the monk, in the scriptorium of Nogent, at the heart of the Middle Ages, during the very first Communes: sensus mentalis. A mental sensation of the events of the world. Thinking is a sense on the same level as scenting or touching. The five senses—in animals—sense *corporaliter*. Thought—in humans—senses *mentaliter*.

Two laws come into conflict in the body: lex mentis and lex peccatis.

This interval of guilt progresses while tearing us apart, hollowing us out from ourselves to ourselves.

Even as 'daimons' had occupied the interval between the earth and the aether for seven centuries, 'peccata' (sins) in medieval Europe until the end of the nineteenth century—until the first couches, until the first patients lay down on the lectus genialis of their conceptio—occupied the interval opened up in the soul.

*

Listening to she who is in front of me means obeying. Ob-audire in Latin, *obaudience* in French: obedience simply means primal listening.

The obsequium was the juridical and social revolution specific to the setting up of the Empire over the Western world some 27 years before the birth of Jesus.

In ancient republican Rome, *subjectus* and *obsequens* were the two epithets which characterized the status of the slave. He is *subjected* to his master and *obedient* to his master's orders under penalty of death.

When Octavian becomes Augustus, the citizen who up to then had been a private father and free man, even before the Roman world had become Christian, became the *obsequious subject*.

Dependence on the inner voice was sacrificed only momentarily during Socrates' sacrifice, to the majority of citizens, in Athens.

An infant hostage of his mother's voice becomes an adult hostage of an inner prescriptive and progressively punitive voice. The English call addiction the state of dependence to which the drug addict has given himself over, independently of the toxicity of the drug that he has chosen as his angel. The revolution of the obsequium during the setting up of the Roman Empire, relayed by Christianism, amplified by States, then by Fascisms, then by Totalitarianisms, developed as addiction to dependence itself.

It is from submission to sound during language learning that sin—a sentiment unthinkable in ancient Rome, as in ancient Greece, as in ancient Egypt—has derived. Obsequiousness is the devastating bond of the lack of obedience to the Voice. Sin is the guilt that causes unrest in the soul of he who contravenes what the divine Voice (Logos, Verbum) orders. This is how the psyche of the Greeks is transformed into the conscience of Westerners. From the ninth to the eleventh centuries, venial sins and mortal sins are gradually differentiated from each other in the souls of those who transgressed the 'commandments' which had made the cephalic cavern their dwelling place and prophesied how to conduct oneself daily.

Then they opposed each other in the inner world, as life and death.

There were four vices in the eyes of the Roman Stoics during the Empire: sadness, desire, fear, joy. Joy was a vice in Rome. Because indestructible solemness and imperturbable austerity were virtues.

Evagrius added madness, fleeing, injustice.

This is how the four vices of the Stoics were gradually transformed into the seven sins of the Christians.

There were seven spirits: life, sight, hearing, smelling, language, taste, procreation.

These spirits, once they went astray (once they 'de-wayed' themselves), became demons who perverted souls. In Stoicism, it was not a matter of extirpating demons, but of de-per-verting demons and of re-con-verting them into spirits.

Left to their demonic nature and having become diabolical, the demons became seven or nine in number, depending on the different codices: lust, gluttony, wrath, coquetry, bewitchment, vainglory, lying, injustice, sleep.

The list of 'mortal' sins was gradually drawn up in turn: adultery, apostasy, murder, sodomy, blasphemy, theft, sacrilege, drunkenness, disobedience.

From the twelfth century until 1941, the Christian hell was the most totalitarian and most appalling machine for crushing the future of each man and each woman that human societies had conceived.

Paradise, purgatory, hell. This is how the three worlds of shamanism came back to Europe in a light which the ancient humans of the prehistoric period, who invented them some 18 millennia beforehand, could never have imagined.

*

In the city of Florence, Antoninius invented something still more invisible and minute: the illness of scrupulosity. He took the Latin word scrupus, which referred to a small rock. He used it to define a persistent microscopic doubt which afflicts the mind, which undermines it with uncertainty, which sinks it into irritation, then in morosity, which paralyses its movements, which sees possible sins everywhere.

The Jansenist Du Guet wrote: At first, the soul is alarm. This worry shows no clarity and does not persuade, but fills the inner world with a disturbing perplexity. One seems to be hearing things inside which cannot be seen outside. It is a *little inner cry*. It is like a glimmer that does not show itself but that warns and goes out. But the means with which one can elucidate a doubt about who knows what? But the means with which one perceives that which allows no entrance into thought to wound or rot there? What one cannot untangle is not necessarily confusing, but thought does not accommodate itself to it. It is like an inexhaustible source whose sound is heard but which is lost in the leaves, a source which one never sees and which immediately replunges its water into the earth.

As Christianism progressively besieged the Empire, it created an unbelievable solicitation of the soul faced with fault.

During the long subjection of the Christian world to the various commandments of its Word, thought became an abnormally unhappy distrust in regard to oneself.

An extraordinarily refined and complex interrogation about the functioning of the mind inside the cephalic cavern.

A *cephalgia*.

A head*ache*.

A virtuoso, casuistic, subtle, flabbergasted, terrified suspicion, obsessed by the eternity of punishments that would be inflicted. When God and the Greek Logos in which he had been incarnated, weakened, dulled, left the Latin language to become diluted in vernacular languages, it was the typically Western invention of psychology that relayed the old penitence and took charge of the survival of this strange 'conscience'. Psychology resulted in psycho-analysis, which substituted itself for the Christian practice of confession when God died in the 1880s, when scientism, Darwinism, the eugenics movement, positivism, futurism, communism, fascism and national socialism began to spread together, competitively, over the surface of the earth. This was the subject—in the addiction to subjection after the secularization of the revolutionary, then, imperial, then democratic worlds—which called for an analyst in a suit, tie and starched collar to replace the spiritual director of conscience (spiritus rector) in a black cassock and white rabat on whom one had relied, up to then, for an interview about one's voices.

Everyone is subject to his anterior State.

Everyone is subject to his inner police.

Everyone is subject to his father and his mother.

Everyone is subject to his Manes.

Reality is more unpredictable than the language that defends us from it.

Reality is more untameable than the world.

Silk comes from a worm, the thread from the cry in the cradle, obedience from the lost voice of the first world, sin from obsequiousness, fright from life, fire from dead branches, human beings from a vulva, the daimon from a mirror, wings from the moon, the angel from masturbation.

CHAPTER 29

The Crossroads

I come back to Socrates. I suspend the conscience that is
born in the imperial Roman world and the destiny of guilt
which will win it over in the Christian world. I return to
thought, no longer to the moment when it says stop, but to
the moment when it gets jammed. In *Meno* 80c, Plato
forcibly describes what he means by the word aporia:
Socrates is a fish that numbs those whom he touches. But
this fish-torpedo-being who numbs (euporon) is himself
petrified (aporon). The first of the philosophers then
declares: 'If I embarrass, then this is because I am myself
embarrassed.' There is a contagion specific to the fact of
being embarrassed, to be stuck in a double bind, to be sunk
into aporia (aporein).

The dialogue does not take place.

The transfer is immobilized.

I is not you, you is not I.

Even as the fascinating and the fascinated—at first perfectly motionless, at first perfectly dying, at first perfectly consenting to die—look at each other, before aggressing each other and before one of them kills the other. Or that both of them—petrified, stalked, terrified—give themselves over to dying on the spot.

*

Plato not only drew the aporia from the depths of halted thinking, but he also brought to light the aporia of the aporia: How can one search for what one does not know?

Plato's response is stupefying: One can search for what one does not know only because there is an originary knowledge. This is anamnesis. The effort consists in remembering the lost. One must already have experienced in order to become acquainted with. It is the zurück effect which founds the emotion of learning. A first realm is needed so that a last realm can reign. And a traumatic scene is needed to move from the former to the latter. This is why each human being goes through the ordeal of the originary. Birth is that ordeal. Birth brings together moving to another place, metamorphosis, the risk of death, the lost object, and, finally, the original knowledge which is the originary distress.

All ulterior knowledge must repose on what the origin says. What the origin 'says' is that which 'cries out' during birth when it discovers pulmonation, the first breath of air into the lungs which sets off the animation of the soul, the aloneness of the sexualized body, the possibility of death, the violence of light.

※

The fascinated recognizes something more ancient than itself in the fascinator. The question 'Why?' has become immobile. This is stupor. The question 'Why?' refers to much more than a mere thirst of knowing (because no substance comes to quench that thirst during a human being's lifetime). If hunger is never sated for more than a few hours, curiosity experiences no diminishing over a period of days, centuries, millennia. The question 'Why?' bears on a reality that goes beyond all that can be known or experienced. The question 'Why?' is addressed by the recent to the ascendance among the ascendants. The subject is this 'hole' (this ante-natal open hole, this originary fissura, this wide-open mouth in the natal cry—this open question, inexhaustibly open, aoristically open, of the erstwhile of one's life, of the world, of the cosmos, of being, of the time relayed in it).

In an individual life, the why is preceded by the newborn animal's astonished gaze at the new world. The astonished gaze of the new on the new is much vaster than a simple 'What's this?'.

Only the autistic person—who does not want to acquire language, who does not want the container to distance itself from him, who especially does not want the upstream to flow away upstream from him, who denies the new, who does not want to hear reality being spoken about—is without why.

The autistic person, the rose, the dawn, the sky are without why.

In the originary times, the unconscious still does not exist (even if there is sleep). But there is a 'knowledge inside the outside' before the unconscious. There is a mysterious 'awaiting' in the nascent (in he who takes part in the unpredictability by surging forth from the origin to arrive in the world). It is a harmonic of container to content, which still proceeds, however, from the repercussivity of a milieu to itself. In the curling of a wave onto itself. A resonance responds to the call before there is a response to this call.

The empty body resounds. Desire already erects itself in that which is famished. The background noise already calls out before the blazing of reality by means of language.

I remember Alain Didier-Weill's big dark apartment in the tenth arrondissement of Paris, along the old canal that leads to the port of the Ourcq. The cats presided. At the end of our discussion, we gave up and let the cats speak; they bowed their heads, and never stopped responding. Alain Didier-Weill's question was: If human reality catches fire like a burning bush in every language, what prevents it (in autism, in insanity), from catching fire? Then our host, next to the empty armchair reserved for the prophet, evoked a mysterious bifurcation: Remain or Become. (No) or yes. (Silence) or language. It was this poor language given to the cats, at least language's simple crying out in the body, the mother's calling out in language, nature's calling out in the sea more ancient than life. But, alas, at this stage, only the yes is possible. The no, the silence, is only blankness, blockage, distress, silence, anorexia, death.

*

This is how I have always remained *ad confinia carnis ac spiritus*. Nothing that I write moves a step away from the border between flesh and thought. I do not intend to cross what I cannot cross. The Last Realm is this singular land in which animal nudity and cultural language perpetually touch each other without ever joining. Guibert the monk was right: Thought is still that *sensus* of the flesh. It is that *aporia*. I did not want to choose. I do not want to choose. I remain in front of the choice.

*

It is Buridan's ass. Either the wild grass or the oats of domestication.

It is Actaeon's stag. Either the goddess or the dog.

*

The emperor Marcus Aurelius (*Meditations* 4.1) brought his life to a halt when facing this dilemma: Either stoicism or epicureanism. Either providence or atoms.

In other words: Either a whole which is a container, a unifying god (in Greek, an enosis) or a scattered impulsive disorder (in Greek, a chaos).

*

The thought that I don't want to express is the fundament of my thought. And the body conceals this thought, which the ego does not know. This is how the natal distress or the trauma that revivifies it deploys each time a strange

pathogenic rumination which has not managed to transform itself into memory or signification. A mysterious
hypermnesia has become stuck and, if it is not without
images, it is without narration. It is truly like a stuck record
in that the motif (the nightmare, the lesion, the incomprehensible moment) is repeated identically, as if knocking on
the door without anything enabling the door to be opened.
There is no password for the languageless—for infancy.

*

King Gilgamesh announces to Uruk: Either a city or the
jungle.

The King of Uruk loves the fortified city whose law he
promulgates, whose crenelated image he places on his hair,
all of whose women he dominates by means of the right he
edicts over them; he loves hunting the wild beasts of the
natural world beyond the walls. However, all of a sudden,
one day, it is love at first sight; he falls in love with a wild
beast while falling in love with Enkidu; he loves he who
dies; he still loves he who has died. He decides to go among
the dead and try to recover his companion. This is the first
novel written in this world, at the end of the fourth
millennium before Jesus Christ.

*

Marcus Aurelius—the great emperor of the second century after Jesus Christ, and the one who killed Saint Blandina—wrote, in Greek, in Rome, in his diary: *Etoi pronoia e atomoi.*

According to the Greek language, such is the deep *crux* of the dilemma. According the Latin language, such is the quadrifurcum of the *crossroads*. Such is the diezeugmenon at every instant of life. Such is the fork (the two branches of the Y) at the heart of every thought.

Either sense or reality.

Either the order of the gods or the rain of atoms.

Either narration or wandering.

*

He who searches (shamana in Sanskrit, zetes in Greek) leaves his wife, his son, his court, the city, enters the pine forest and wanders there for eternity, in the perpetual frustration of his desire.

*

Sappho, the great poetess of the Greek world, in fragment 51: I don't know what to run towards. Two projects are in me. Duo moi ta noemata.

Two in me are thoughts.

I am divided (mermerizo), that is, I am divided as if in two parts (meros) that oppose each other. This is how thought rises in her before she throws herself off Cape Lefcada into the sea.

*

In ~408, in Argos, Menelaus does not know whether he should support Orestes' cause or should follow the judgement just brought to him by Tyndareus. Orestes urges him to make his decision.

'Menelaus, where is your thought going while you pace back and forth, following, one after the other, two divergent worries?'

'Leave me. Leave me, Orestes', the hesitating king responds, murmuring. 'I am thinking. Nothing resolves itself in me. *I don't know what is thinking what I am thinking.*'

*

The Vedic competition of the brahmodhya was a competition of enigmas in order to provoke a shock (a fire) of unanswerable questions. It is the joy of unfathomable interrogation. And the transcendence of deafening silence (in Sanskrit, brahman) which results in the depths of the body.

*

There are aspects of reality to which one can accede if and only if others are missing.

One cannot enjoy sexual pleasure by opening one's eyes.

Any vision x is a blindness y.

Any audition Y is a deafness x.

Whoever scents does not taste.

Whoever listens does not spring forth.

One cannot sleep while standing.

One does not love someone if one thinks of oneself.

CHAPTER 30

About Concepts of Things

The Romans preferred to call conceptus that which we call the foetus. Colour photographs that are taken of embryos inside their mother's abdomen show small beings who live all cuddled up in their private pouch. To say this in Latin, these little *conceptus* are tucked away in their *uterus*. Their minute body is incurved, their arms are curled up, their legs are contracted, their eyes are closed. This is how even the conceptus in the amniotic water keep their eyelids extremely squinted shut and act like beings who are dreaming. They protect their face behind their marvellous translucent frog-like fingers. Such are therefore concepts.

Macrobius long compared the intellectual representation which seeks to take form, which endeavours to develop its arguments in the depths of the mind of the mature human being, to the little embryonic body that is growing and expanding and singularizing its organs in the tepid, euphoric water that the maternal abdomen contains in an enclosed, long locked-up and essentially waterproof skin pouch.

*

Noetics, he noetike techne, defines the art of making concepts surge forth. Maieutics or midwifery, he maieutike techne, defines the art of delivering babies. In Greek, the maieuma which results from this refers to the newborn, in the same way that noema refers to the content of thought. This is how the Greek noeme is called in Latin conceptus and leads to the French and English concept. The content of thought is a 'conceived' of the mind.

Maieusis refers to the *upending* active metamorphosis of delivering a baby from women—not only onto the ground but also into the light—which is social reproduction itself. Maieusis, which renews human societies, refers to the natal pain, to the intrusive, pneumatic, sonorous, bloody violence, even as the noesis, which indicates the attentive movement of thinking, refers to the psychic contention and tragic wrenching between two hostile theses which perpetually confront each other.

The maieutria or 'midwife' is the 'sage' woman (*sage-femme*), and this sagacity referred, from the origin, to the 'sage' contained in 'philo-sophos', that is, he who 'loves the sage'. But if the *sage-femme* was chosen by Socrates because it was his mother, this philo-sage omits to say that his father, like genesis itself (the genetics before sexual reproduction), *sculpted*. For there is a prelinguistic symbolic. There are two paths: images and words, even as there are two worlds which are the fruits of the sexuation of humanity sectioned off between men and women. In Latin, it is the stone sax, in the depths of the sectio, which divides humanity into its two sexes, one hollowed out, the other protrus, which are themselves in perpetual confrontation. There is a sexual Erstwhile before the Before. Then there is a Before (before the inside/outside of the second pulmonated world). This is the first world. This is the mother as a container. Then there is a Referent (before the signifier/signified division of oral language) and it is the lost mother. It is the mother as another body, as an object in the second world, after birth and the cry before the breath. This is why it is likely that projective identification is the first thought. It is a noesis before being a noema. It is a hunt for what one loses. A quest for that of which one is the loser. Contents project themselves towards the Container, towards the Nourisher, towards the Mother, towards the mother's breasts, towards Mother's nourishment, towards the mother's thought, towards the mother's erstwhile.

*

It is only in the oeuvre of Saint Thomas Aquinas—before his thought collapses at the end of the year 1273—that the conceptus began to leave the gestation inside the body of the mother. The word conceptus, once written, was decomposed and tended to be etymologized. Paradoxically, it was inverted as it was etymologized, de-molecularized, archaeologized. Thomas Aquinas writes: Con-ceptus con-capit. The 'taken together' takes together. A concept brings together (different elements into a unique mode). A concept can thus be defined as a unity of original thought which forgets its hallucinatory origin, which considers itself to be completely intentional and significative, which does not derive from the outside world, which is born in the mind, which concentrates traits that have never been brought together until then. Thomas Aquinas specifies in *De rationibus fidei* 3: When it seeks to comprehend (intellegere), the intellect forms an intelligible which is, as it were, its *child* (proles) and which, for this reason, is called the *foetus of thought* (conceptus mentis).

*

Whatever we think, our thoughts do not belong to us. No more than we are at the source of our body, we are not at the source of our hallucinations nor are the dedicants of our wishes nor are the masters and tamers of our desires. Whatever efforts we make, the wrinkling of our forehead, the wrinkling of our eyebrows, the cohesive focusing of our eyes, attentiveness and application are not of a voluntary nature. They come from Elsewhere. They come from the

Referent. Thought never ceases to make bonds going back to the first symbolic.

Legere is relegere. The logos, or the religio, means binding with the lost.

'What are you thinking of?'

'Nothing.'

And, indeed, one cannot say what one is thinking of *because it is with the lost that one thinks.*

'Whom are you thinking of?'

'Of nothing precise because I have lost it. Of what has been lost in me.'

The noesis cannot be its own noema in the same way as the delivery cannot be the newborn.

CHAPTER 31

The Aesthetics of Thought

There is a sensation (in Greek, an aesthesis) of thought. Thought, said the monk Guibert of Nogent, is a sense among senses, a scenting specific to the soul, a tact that has its own contact inside the world. The noesis experiences something that it specific to it, calls to something that is specific to it, enters into a relation with something that is specific to it, evolves in something that is specific to it, curls up in a hiding place that is specific to it or, rather, clings on in a pouch that it secretes rather in the way that an egg creates the secret solitary space of its own pouch. It constructs a refuge specific to its hallucination in order to bring back the sexual orgasm that was at its origin.

Every genuine thought is a short-circuit in the shadows. The hand rises to the forehead to shelter the eyes. The eyelids rumple, bunch up, wrinkle. The forehead creases. Inner life is this incurvation of a line which either loops back on itself (conscience, retrogradation, guilt) or suddenly touches itself like two wires with opposite electric charges (thought, illumination).

Conceptio therefore indicates a 'shorter' short-circuit with respect to the psychic circulation of the acquired language.

What is a 'short' circuit? A short-circuit is a surprising, sudden, almost non-deductible contact that transmits.

What is this surprising, sudden, almost non-deductible contact that transmits? Coition. During coition, the bringing into contact of the sexual differences is that which reproduces the embryonic whole in time and the concept in space. Coition is the conception of the human body at its origin.

The *coire-coïtare*, which makes up the originary phantasm, is the first co-agitation in the depths of the infant's cogito.

What is at stake is to re-join the original activity in which all the works in the auto-dissimulation of their functioning and in the unpredictability of their ends are improvised.

But this live communication is neither coition nor birth. If being born and thinking are contemporaneous, each of them drawing directly from the brutal loss of the first world, coition and birth are never simultaneous.

It is, moreover, this human impossibility (that of a simultaneity between erection, coition, conception, parturition, nativity) which presided over the invention of the

Virgin Mary's virginity, leading to an *immaculate* 'conceptio' of a divine 'conceptus' falling from the sky.

This myth, which concerns theologians, dreams of a
birth contemporaneous with the origin.

In the condition of each and every one of us, viviparity
is the core of the desynchrony. We have two lives, which we
lead in two worlds. Desynchrony is the ordeal of time. And
we go backwards: We are augurs who move from tonitrua
to fulgura. We pass from the thunderclap to the flash of
lightning. We go from the realm of shadow to the realm of
light. For the third time in this book, which is, however,
more devoted to thought than to metamorphosis, I meet up
again with Apuleius. It was once again this thinker and
novelist who—in Carthage, in 157—created in Latin the
adjective 'viviparus'. He himself specifies that he has created
the word viviparous by seeking to translate the epithet
'zootokos' employed by the Athenians.

Two times or tempos give rhythm to the phantom scene
from which our two lives proceed: 1. Noema: reinforcing
the invisible sexual embrace from which our body derives.
2. Noesis: the effort of thinking remobilizes Issir, Nativity
(Christmas for Christians, Mars for Romans). The name
given to this active anteriority that dreams of itself as the
origin before the conception and as the conception before
the birth matters little. Thought in its raw, brutal state,
thought which has become brutal, indicates the paradox:

that which leaves an anterior world. Doxa which breaks with the doxa. Noeme which defies the noesis. A paradox refers to a short-circuit by which a normal, regular, habitual, traditional, predictable consecution fuses. A logical sequence—or a liturgical, maniacal, mulled-over moral—short-circuits and this delights the listener's soul. Noëmon is the name of a warrior in Virgil *Aeneid* 9.767. By writing the name of Noëmon, I think that I am transcribing the Japanese patronym of a shadowy hero who haunts the nightly world while searching for his murderer. The thinker wages a tragic combat in that he desperately seeks to resynchronize two worlds. Thought relays the old sexual embrace, the originary confrontation, between two 'differents', which concludes in the unpredictable orgasmic annihilation.

The aorist 'Eureka!' for which every researcher searches, following Archimedes on the slope of his volcano, endlessly repeats this invisible scene in the background of the visible, which never reaches sight, and which abruptly escapes in a dream, in a phantasm, in thought amid the ruins of a bombed or burnt-down city.

Catastrophic surfacing of the pleasure which rises, catastrophically, in the soul as a strange death which one wishes more than anything else in the world.

*

Plato wrote in his *Letter* 7.341d: *as suddenly as a light appears at the instant that the flame flares up*, existence is irradiated by the thought that results from the inner experience that has prepared it for days, seasons, years.

The All-of-a-Sudden presupposes the unappeased erection even as every dream shows along the way the lack of that which it puts forth as an image.

Plato's favourite Greek adverb—exaiphnes, suddenly— is the temporal sign introducing one to knowledge of a third kind, which is pure happiness. A joy that spurts forth.

Time accelerates in the noetic insight as it does in the anticipation and the extreme proximity of sexual voluptuousness.

All comprehension chronically catches time off-guard in its consciousness as well as in its anticipation. This is how a temporal experience, which is comparable to that of speed in space, takes place in thought at the moment when the neuronal system integrates a new relation. The brain *senses* this sudden promptitude inside the cephalic cavity to the extent that the basso continuo of the inner world (the heartbeat) is affected by it.

Was heist Denken? It is a kind of physics. There is a marvellous physics of thought. With the noun Aha-Erlebnis, Karl Bühler indicated the experience that is pensive, then suspensive, then saltatory, then exalting, of any animal who abruptly discovers, in his hunt for nourishment, a new solution for capturing. Instinct is not at stake, but rather a kind of Eureka. A kind of Erstwhile from which the beast *rushes*. Similarly, Archimedes, after the aoristic cry, *rushes* (inasmuch as his body is *lifted* by the excitation of the discovery, he first wants to note it down to recall it before communicating it to all those who will be able to comprehend it). An *orient* is suddenly discovered from that which is non-oriented—an orientation that *precipitates* it. From this, an effect of speed, which is a polarization of the field. The excitation erects the sexual organ, makes it swell, accelerates the rhythm (in Latin, the pulsio; in French, the *pouls*; in English, the pulse) of the heart. Emerging from the depths of consciousness is something entirely new which is propagated at high speed from neuron to neuron, taking along with it all the ancient elements, which it recomposes. This is how noetic activity acts as a motor before it becomes an authentic emotion of the soul.

*

At night, the fulguration of lightning that a storm brings along with it through the sky is another originary image of this motivity. It is really a grandiose spectacle of physics. And it is truly a beauty that is each time renewed, unpredictable and certain. Lightning dashing from peak to peak.

A flash of radiance in the night of the cephalea. An epiphany because of the ignition of an outside element that appears by chance.

The divine invading the self was literally called enthousiasmos. The in-corporation of the god in oneself. What is other invades the inner world exactly like the air which devastates at top speed, all of a sudden (with a sudden cry), the volume of the body at the moment of birth.

What cannot be anticipated joins up with the unmatchable (fish and air) and synchronizes all of a sudden on a new basis (the upright posture running at top speed on two feet, after the act of swimming). This is trans-port itself: the meta-phora. Two allogenic elements violently sym-bolize, as at the origin. What cannot be anticipated by what is anterior rushes like a content into a container. This is the trans-fer. It takes up all the place in the volume offered by the body even as water widens and distends a pouch that has become enthusiastic.

Suddenly surges forth—exaiphnes—in the noesis a meta-noesis. One can translate the Greek word 'metanoia' by psychic turnover, by the reversal of the mind. This is what preached John the Converter, the Nomothetes, the Baptist, on the Jordan—sinking the body of god himself into the water of the first world. In Greek, John calls this baptism 'metanoia'. With this, one once again comes across

King Redbad, with whom these pages began—his foot
hovering over the water. In Greek, this is an epoche. In
Latin, a suspensio. King Redbad is in an aporia. With Jesus,
the short-circuit is consummated. Redbad turns away from
the baptism. Jesus is immersed. This meta-noia (this thought
beyond) was translated into Latin by the word 'con-versio'.
A new thought is at once conversion and rebirth. The 'converted' person is reborn into another life. He is therefore
like a re-infant, like a re-nascent, like a re-born. His pleasure
is purely inner. It is en-thusiastic. It is this involuted pleasure, without genital satisfaction, that the monks of tantrism
have so eloquently described, for 2,000 years, in the caves
of the mountains of Tibet. Intrapsychic voluptuousness: the
sperm suddenly rising to the brain. Infinite autoerotic
research about the origin of the body in the body.
Impossible originary thought. Empty lookout of the aporia.
Curiosity without an outcome. The begging of this inexplicable nirvana—such is the neophyte's tireless quest near
his master whose psyche has become empty.

*

The Latin verb cogito can be de-composed into this form:
actus mentis co-agans in lingua. This inner co-agitation of
the psyche (of the breath that animates the body) with

language (the spoken language which is itself acquired in a desynchronized way with respect to the psychic birth, that is, with respect to the intrusion of air into the body) is the basis of thought, of writing, of delirium, which is like a dream co-agitated by the painfully acquired national language which short-circuits thought and overwhelms the inner world during perception, hallucination, somnambulism, insane action, truth in person, the fides taking action.

A linguistic co-agitation inside the body—such is, at first, all thought halfway between what is dreamt and intellection. The infantile brain, as it is painfully converted, over a long period of time, to language, as it becomes puerile, as it begins to believe in the world born of language, as it grows from its own random playing, prolongs the dream, disengages itself from heredity or, at least, distends its genetic programming, invents an unknown sensoriality (mind), puts in place a curiosity that weaves and claims to re-unite (inter-legere, which founds intelligence), imposes the recognition of an All behind reality (a mother making the pieces of time merge), hallucinates a unity behind acts (a force, a demon, a mind, a soul), organizes a sojourn for the elements of time that it represses (memory), attempts an incessant, initially muscular, then visual, finally linguistic and mnemonic re-totalization of experience (consciousness).

Winnicot clearly distinguished states of non-integration and states of disintegration. To him, the former seemed capable of being experienced with pleasure (solitude, aporetic thought). This was not the case with the latter (abandonment, delirious confusion). As to Freud, he thought that anything unbound was unwell, was suffering. To his mind, the fragmentary was always the saddening fruit of a ruin or mourning. Therefore, all the aftermath of an orphanhood, whatever its nature, seemed destined for melancholy. Deleuze thought like Freud. Any chaos was malaise and only philosophy was good. I doubt that this is the case. Although there is a laetitia specific to thought that integrates its new conceptus, there is also the crazy joy of disintegration. A possible ecstasy of that which is pathless, a dead end, aporos, problematic, incertus, vagus. A meta-noesis. An explosivity. A curiosity taking action and in fact relaying the primitive animal alertness and its endless state of being on the lookout.

It is this joy that turned me away from philosophy.

Reading is born of this disintegration of oneself inside another self. At first, there is a difficult disintegration (one must 'get into' the novel), which is followed by a marvellous merging during the reading (one can no longer leave the novel).

No longer inside reading, but inside *nature*, there is an ecstasy during contemplation (theoria) in which the body, up to then personal, becomes a part of that which it contemplates.

Colette was the only author to have thought of the rancour of nature with respect to the human world. She was the only one to have thought of the sensorial reclamation of the originary earth as it faces the linguistic world: the silent, fundamental grievance of the elements, of plants, of insects, of shellfish, of fish, of birds, of all the exterminated animals in regard to the gluttony of men and women. The terrifying ogre of fairy tales is a humanity become enormous over the surface of the earth. Hunger rips apart. Desire *binds* or, rather, because the liaison is anterior to pleasure whereas the tension of desire orientates and re-binds, the coition explodes during the voluptuous ejaculation. Coition is the source of the neuronal, then verbal, relation (in the same way that it is at the source of the body sheltering such relations). This is why we are interested in thinking by means of joy itself. That which re-binds maintains the excitation, provides the sense, de-chaotizes the suffering in order to be able to go, in company of the liaison (co-ire), towards the pleasure that is its genuine orient, where it is re-chaotized. As to sexual pleasure, it *unbinds* absolutely.

*

The German word nachträglich means afterwards. The distinctive feature of analytical experience is this 'suddenly afterwards'. For this 'suddenly afterwards' defines a 'rethinking unexpectedly, all of a sudden, of everything that has been experienced'. This attempt to rethink of everything in a language that is no longer outer but inner, no longer spoken but written—such is literature. Each genuine oeuvre rethinks of everything that has spoken, reanimates everything that has become breathless, been smothered, repressed, strangled and snuffed out.

To Sigmund Freud's mind, the first period of time is not only misunderstood, insane, but it also incessantly shipwrecks, body and goods, into the depths of the body. This why a second time is needed so that the first time can resurge from the waves, or from shadow, or from pain, or from silence. In love, the *coup de foudre* (love at first sight, as if struck by a thunderbolt) is the expression for this second time. This second time is suddenly reattached to the inherence of origin—to the fusional inherence. For Jacques Lacan, that which has not been admitted into the symbolic reappears in reality. In all cases, the first period of time is absent: in Freud, absent from memory; in Lacan, from symbolization. To use the more precise terms that they liked to employ, the 'retroactive phantasm' in Freud (the Zurückphantasieren) and the 'denegation' in Lacan (the foreclosure or, in French, the *forclusion*) seek to think of this same wave movement which folds back on itself before the spoken language. An advance that is a retreat. First realm and last realm.

Fois and *autrefois*—'time' and 'in other times'.

Coup and *après coup*—'blow' and 'after the blow', 'that is, (all of a) sudden' and 'afterwards'.

⁎

Going from the void to fullness. Going from fullness to the void. It is possible to make a game out of a delirium and to dig into study all the way down to the ruins.

It is possible to make a last realm out of a bad symptom.

A rereading out of a delirium.

⁎

In times past, were there by chance a few human beings who got involved, body and soul, inside their thought in order to experience it? To the period of un-excitability, which follows upon the desiring world, must be added the nervous depression that confronts the resourceless person. The hilflos, the aporos, the masochist, the oblat and the depressive person almost see reality with a naked eye. Emptiness. Zhuang Zhou, Heraclitus, Gorgias, Ovid, Petronius, Apuleius, Abelard, Petrarch, Montaigne, Descartes, La Fontaine, Spinoza, Rousseau, Bataille—all of them knew how to invent an implicant form. All of them had to face this *folding back,* this *falling back*—this *withdrawal*—into the void. Most of them had to leave all their functions within social functioning; some ended up killing themselves; or were excommunicated; or went into exile. The groups to which they belonged crafted for them tailor-made, denigrating legends about their asocial personalities. *Vitae* of anchorites. Heraclitus stoned by children in the mountains, Lucretius in tears killing himself out of love, Montaigne unaware of the number of his daughters, Rousseau abandoning his children without even giving them names, Bataille offering his wife and his daughter to Lacan. Spinoza was excommunicated from the Amsterdam synagogue; he didn't even dare to show *Ethica* to his best friends; he died, probably assassinated by the French. By order of the emperor, Petronius was forced to kill himself. Abelard was castrated and his book was burnt. Ovid was exiled and imprisoned in a tower at the end of the human world, at the mouth of the Danube, where the interminable river empties into the Black Sea. Descartes—the least French, and probably the best, of all the French philosophers—spending his entire life fleeing France and dying in the snow.

CHAPTER 32

On the Radiation of Thought

Listen to people sighing! Sighing means snuffing out a candle in the depths of the soul.

Freud wrote: The dominant tendency of psychic life aims at suppressing the tension of excitation. In his office in Vienna and without much reason, Freud then uses a Sanskrit word: nirvana. Extinction. This word belongs to Buddhism. Snuff out the candle. Suppress suffering, illusion, desire. But is what Freud asserts, true?

I am not so sure.

The search for tension is also a genuine passion. One can detest the pleasure, the death, the un-excitability and the nausea into which voluptuousness plunges the assuaged body. One can make gods of extreme erections, hunger, vigilance, desire and tension. Cats like nervous tension. It attracts them like a kind of warmth, like a movement of waves, like a sort of electricity. Cats irresistibly approach motionless, troubled, worried beings—or even beings who are themselves approaching death with the greatest stupor.

PASCAL QUIGNARD

Cats climb onto those who are intensely and silently searching for their words, for their order in the sentence, with their fingers clenching the end of a pencil. They stretch out their entire length on the bodies of those dreaming of something that they do not yet know how to articulate. The increase in this tension of desire, in this concentration of energy, impassions psychic life as much as it magnetizes cats towards the flesh which, in its silence, afflicts and attracts them. Like a ray of sunlight magnetizes them on the shelf where they have positioned themselves, having early on sleeked up on it. Or on the edge of the roof illumined by the sunlight between the leaves of the trees. It feels good to rest one's body there, as if near a fire in a fireplace which has suddenly, curiously, the appearance of a roof tile, a slate board, a page or a human being. For it is not the writer who loves cats, or cats which love writers. Cats love thought.

*

At the end of the night, when the cats leave their cushions, when right out of the blue they renounce the bowl of water that shines in the shadow on the red tiles of the kitchen, when they move past the bowl full of croquettes without looking at it, when they climb on their velvety paws the steps of the stairway leading to the bedroom, when they push the door with their foreheads or lower the door handle

202

with a stroke of their paws, they do not climb up on the bed, nor stamp on the torso of their master to wake him, although this is the disturbing or irritating impression that we have every dawn; they have detected from very far away sleep coming to a halt; they catch the neurological re-starting-up in the very act. Sensing that the radiator of thought has begun to heat up again, they cannot tolerate our pretending to sleep or our seeking to fiddle away a few extra seconds from the necessity of getting up. Then, a neurological connecting up takes place from brain to brain; not from signification to signification; but from cerebral activity to cerebral activity. Cats detect the electricity of wakefulness from afar (before the body is present in the room). They grasp. (For example, from the kitchen to the office, they perceive from a distance, and begin trotting from there.) They head for the place where thought is warmest. Mental concentration hails their prancing body. The mental activity of their master, or of another cat, or of anyone or anything (a fearful little field mouse, a trembling squirrel), beckons to them like a magnetic pole. The agitation of thought (in Latin the e-motio of the co-agitato; in Greek the energeia of the noesis) makes them happy. They are perfectly indifferent to the contents of thought (the noemes). The electric effervescence of the other body is like a warm earthenware stove, a big cast-iron radiator through which water gurgles and near which they feel good. Near which their life is under tension, and the relation re-joined. They position their elbows, tuck away their paws, either ball up or stretch themselves out; it is as if they were in their mother's stomach; they can sleep confidently near a being whose gigantic vigilance protects them.

*

Bêtise—stupidity: being as stupid as an animal, as a beast—is not the forte of animals. The *bêtes* (animals) are not *bêtes* (stupid). They embody such immediateness, such motivity, such reactivity, such dance, that no distance could make their stupidity appear above their instinct. Stupidity defines the *hominizing source* of animals no longer wishing to be animals. Stupidity is the unfathomable residual which betrays human beings in regard to their own extraction. Their stupidity is incessant, both a continuous leftover coming back from the past and the ineffaceable evidence of a betrayal. Stupidity haunts humanity. It is that from which human beings want to differentiate themselves at all costs. It is the vulgar and bloody and savage and animal and famished and murderous shame of their inappeasable origin.

Science is a wellspring of legends even more hypo-thetical than myths themselves. Our brain is a sedimentation of the past of all the stages of animality. The so-called archaic brain dates back to ~500 million years. It is the brain of instincts or functions. The brain of fish, frogs, turtles. It responds, to the milieu, by functions that are cardiac, then respiratory, then nutritional, then sexual.

The so-called paleomammalian brains dates back to ~180 million years. It responds, to the milieu, by fear, and to fear by the regular death that one calls sleep until the final sleep. This life of fear, which is rhythmed by a state of being on the lookout that exhausts the body, sinks the brain rhythmically into a sleep that repairs it. The primary motions and emotions of the body are aggression, fleeing, submission to the group, oneiric abandonment.

The cortex called neocortex, which is much more recent, deals with information coming from the outer world (by five or six or seven or eight senses) and information ensuing from the inner world (by feedback or through memory). It falls within the province of dreaming and night. It is the headquarters of thought, of language, of memory, of conscience, of lies, of secrets. The lateralization of the superior mammals and the acquisition of articulated language by human beings have specialized the right cerebral hemisphere of right-handed people into the perception of time (synthesis). Lateralization and the acquisition of language have specialized the left cerebral hemisphere into the function of language, logic and symbolism (analysis).

This is why rhythms, durations and the great scale of time are incomprehensible to the acquired language. Thrusts, waves, rhythms, undulations and modulations are immediately accessible only to the right, ancient, archaic cerebral hemisphere—to the old musician of erstwhile who does not speak but who dreams and who sings and who follows in the water—like a pike, a carp, a moray eel—the undulations of the wave which goes by and that weighs down on him, which envelops him and which he suckles. This is why the body is the originary archive in action. This is why the brain, in every instant of its functioning, sets off the tripartite aorist of the evolution of its metamorphosis. Our genes preserve the memory of erstwhile. The chemical composition of each of our cells is a part of the primitive ocean. The milieu from which we come speaks, within each of us, in its strange dialect.

This is why I had to put forward an Erstwhile more contemporary than the past.

What is the past? The universe. The *response* given by the universe before any possible linguistic questioning suggests the *a posteriori* (nachträglich) question of the erstwhile. Memory is a past whereas sleep is an erstwhile. This is a mysterious legacy of evolution. The dense, unconscious, incredible experience of sleeping. An enigmatic phase of genetic reprogramming and of chaos the enchanter. Of the reanimation of that which occurs in the present, not through past acts, but through the origin. The erstwhile revisits the body every night *to cleanse it of the past.*

In the ordering of periods of time, human History is merely the terrible face of compulsive repetition. But there is no history of the erstwhile. The erstwhile never stops beginning to begin. Phylogenesis washes down ontogenesis, cleans all the corners, the slightest bit of plinth, moves all the furniture, lifts the rug.

The origin cleans History even as animality cleans stupidity.

*

One changes pasts with every love. As the soul associates itself with the anecdotes of the different soul, whose body discovers the different body in its overwhelming genital nudity, the soul is at once swept away by perpetual curiosity and oriented by the new, specific desire that it provokes.

The soul discovers the different soul in the old enchantment of the first voice heard in the water, under the water, beyond the water, muffled by the originary penumbra.

In the 1830s, during the riots that followed Molé's fall from power, the extraordinary Chateaubriand of *Memories from Beyond the Grave* was called the 'old enchanter'. Such is love, born with the acquired language. Then each person tells his or her life to the other person so differently that it is new. Each time, this enchantment is a re-enchantment drawing on a chant even older than its atmospheric modulation. Older than any human language.

*

With each novel, the novelist changes pasts.

Such is the nature of the past: it changes, whereas no one changes the erstwhile. The erstwhile has no time that can be changed: it surges forth without ever ending.

*

Immobile, in the middle of the crossroads, not knowing which road to take, like King Oedipus.

Immobile, at the edge of the vat, meditating on his dead ones, like King Redbad.

In thought, the epoche does not consist, in the first place, of 'suspending' judgement like the sense that the word has taken on in philosophical reflexion. The epoche at first consists of remaining in the originary aporia; of persisting to search for an access in the access-less. It means resisting opinion (dogma) by continuing to search.

In *Metaphysics* 995a35, Aristotle speaks of 'searching in the aporia' and not of 'suspending judgement'. Thinking in the sense of meditating means contemplating the impossible situation inside the aporia. The thinker is obstinate until he inhabits the thaumazein: this astonishment, which refers to the celestial storm, is contemplation itself. As a movement of petrified alarm, a sensation of radical incomprehensibility, it is more than a kind of wisdom: it is an immobile ecstasy.

But how can one come back into reality without being transformed by this movement of backwardation and secession?

How can belonging and being in an 'unbelonging' return be broken?

Scepticism does not belong to the philosophy of the ancient Greeks of Athens.

In the ancient world, scepticism proceeded directly from the Buddhism of the ancient Indians present in Mediterranean trading posts. The pleasure of isosthenia is not shared by all human beings. It is the pleasure of giving equal value to opposing arguments, then of giving them no more value. The pleasure of aporia is an aphasia. The pleasure of not judging, of not discriminating, of not asserting, is Satori.

*

Whereas the East ecstatically enjoys sexual pleasure, the West is depressive. Whereas the Resourceless is abruptly nirvana, the Helpless is sensed as genuine distress. Acedia and Hilflosigkeit are the Manes of Europe. Nervous depression and the originary distress have formed, from the Roman world to the sumptuous maturity of the Christian world, the vertigo of Europe. The very idea of the Middle Ages, of a subsided and sinister transition (between the Roman Empire and modern States) characterizes European history. Europe is a civilization at the heart of which beats, as a heart pulses, a terrible collapse in which it closes itself up as if in a hell. This collapse is purely imaginary, but Europe believes in it. For Christians, human life is a hell from which one must exit by death in order to re-join immortality and eternity. Europe *produced* this hell, before *plunging* its history into this hell that it had invented.

*

A thinker lives for the pleasure not only of a faithless search, but also of a causeless quest. In this sense, a thinker is the opposite of an intellectual. Pure interrogation (without knowledge, without commitment, without an ideal, without opinion, without expectation, without conviction, without belief, without a mission, without accreditation, without authorization, without a wage or salary, without a country).

*

It is true that the epoche—at the heart of the aporia—is a vertiginous social attitude: non-consent to the majority, non-obedience to the language, thought like a state of alertness in which all consensus, all synthesis, all hope, all sense, are lost.

It means remaining, trembling like a leaf, face to face with what one does not know rushing towards you.

*

Sextus Empiricus wrote marvellously: Don't search for ecstasy. Don't turn it into an outcome. Likewise, don't make distress into an ordeal. Don't make a passage even out of meaninglessness. There is no ultimate stage in the potential experience of human beings. Don't bend over; don't bend your face towards the depths of thought; there is nothing to reach in the depths of thought. The noesis is without a noeme. The res cogitans is a substance without an object like the first world. Even as hunger is empty, from which the res cogitans derives during dreaming, this élan is endless. Let the élan ease up. Let wind, breath, air, transparency, daylight come in and go out as they wish. Don't close the door or the window if your intention is to keep the cat with you; you will make it furious. Leave the window leaf perpetually half-open so that the cat can push it with the end of its paw and then it will remain at the foot of your bed or at the end of the cover on your bed, and it will gently place its cheek on the end of its furry, withdrawn fingers, and it will fall asleep without worry near the soul who thinks and trembles.

*

The ancient Greeks paradoxically spoke of a 'dynamis antithetike'. The power of a parataxis of immobile contradictories. Antithesis is not a kind of reasoning: it means putting equal forces into combat. The interlocking of bull horns in a Roman arena, the clashing and entanglement of deer antlers in a November forest—such is the essence of the ancient epoche. It is the combat of desires which confront each other on a November night. The ataraxia of ancient sceptics is the opposite of rest; it is the biggest erection; it is *tension that is equally violent, everywhere, infinite.*

CHAPTER 33

Aseitas

Any thought is never all thought. The reproduction of the species through sexuality implies that half of humanity neither knows what the other half thinks nor how it thinks. One can say: 'The deepest thought is always lacking 50 per cent of the capacity of anthropological thinking.' Thought is partial, biased, always sexually differentiated, in generic disagreement, in generational divergence, in social conflict, in linguistic opposition. Each thought is, at best, merely one of two possible thoughts. The fact that the deliberation at the heart of thought only acknowledges the sexuation-origin has consequences that are quickly vertiginous; the sexuation-origin is dissonant, anti-mythic, anti-semantic, disunifying, rending. It is not only hostilizing, but also immediately omni-conflictual. There is no originary unity: those who made us were two in number. There is no aseity: we do not come from ourselves. This is Heraclitus' intuition, at the end of the Neolithic world, on the Turkish shore of

Europe. The absence of unity and the lack of aseity imply that there is no eschatological meaning. There is not *one* Urlogos, *one* metalanguage, *one* UrHistoria, *one* God, *one* metachrony, *one* future. Not even *one* synchrony and not even *one* past. There are only two 'one's', neither one nor the other (neither truly one nor truly other) face to face. Un (masculine case) and *une* (feminine case). Distinct but not even opposed. The identification indicates only this: a 'not-wholly-one-and-not-wholly-other' claims to make a self (claims to seize, assimilate, devour) a 'quasi-other'. A really unreal one. Neither ever a whole, never ever a couple. This fissuration, this cut, this trait, this literal mark denuded of sense, this pre-literary letter, this sexus is one: a 'one' which is never the same on each person. Such is the ever-imaginary heart of the letter. This letter appears neither on the body of the man nor on that of the woman because it makes a sign to what of one is not on the other and to what of the other is not on she who reproduces the same and the non-same from her unique sexual organ. Language hops from stone to stone in order to dialogue, like society from body to body in order to reproduce itself while strangely limping on only one of its poles. The most originary language is this poor incessant difference, which reproduces little ones, a section without parity which cannot be immobilized, a difference so insignificant, so abstract and never graspable, that nothing, however, reduces, from which one keeps turning away one's eyes but which the eyes always keep quickly questioning with uneasiness.

*

Die Wahrheit wird euch frei machen. Such is the German motto which is regilded every 10 years on the rose-coloured fronton of the University of Freiburg. But truth does not make us free. The depths of the hallucinated psyche. The depths of language, like the depths of the soul, assembles hallucinations, hungers, desires, dreams, phantoms of those who are dead, lies, incomprehensible alterities, apprenticeships, dependencies.

*

The locus of the unreal among the ancient Normans was called Gleipnir. This invisible territory is made up of the noise of cat steps, of the beard that falls from the cheeks of little girls, of the roots of mountains, of the antlers that grow on the foreheads of bears, of the breath of birds.

*

In every ego, there is a little more species than individual, a little more genus than species, a little more animality than humanity, a little more of everything than of parts, a little more of reality than of everything.

A little less of two and a little more of one in this two that each body divides.

To my mind, it is not the intelligible (the noeton) which makes up the object of the thought (of the noos) originating from the language (the logos), but the 'letting the unintelligible be' of all the senses (before their signification and before their opposition within the logos before the learning of the maternal language). It is the hilflos, the logos-los, the in-fans of the discovery of the incomprehensible human world.

There is an im-participable.

That which is before the acquiring of language is an im-participable.

When philosophy refers everything to the philological logos which searches, what thinking thinks simply refers to this im-participable from which the body proceeds, to this un-domesticable that language pushes back, to this non-thetic which obsesses the oldest meditations in the world.

The premises are outside the soul, originary in the depths of time and stubborn in the depths of the mind which has never perceived them or which has been unable to retain them due to a lack of verbal traces to repatriate them from the depths of time where language does not exist. We know almost nothing about these premises even if they remain deep inside ourselves. Finally, it must be acknowledged that the evaluation of the nature of the unknown is itself empirical.

It happens that dreams, thought experiences, novels, phantasms are capable of offering an a priori acquaintance with nature. We construct mental representations from a constructive depth older than ourselves. The mind has its abysses in which a strange, little-known life moves: famished, dreamt, pensive hallucination and meditation pursue them. Galileo while thinking, Kant while thinking, Einstein while thinking relayed something of which the empirical experience was probably not absurd but of which they were nonetheless the test. Mathematics draws its truth from an a priori depth which it would be difficult to derive uniquely from culture or from anthropology. One must think this: If there is no time outside of language, it is the virtual itself which is originary.

*

Reality is not true. It is more savage than the true.

Physics and mathematics are perhaps allogenic contemplations.

Physics and philosophy are surely allogenic.

Seneca is clear. *Seneca ad Lucilium* 14: the object of philosophy is human social assembly.

What is true of philosophy (whose history one must consider as beginning with Socrates wanting to die in the city that is persecuting him) is not true of thought (for example, Zhuang Zhou or Heraclitus, in both of whose minds the thinker is apolis and every thinker's life a perpetual escape from palaces, from courts, from bourgs).

Seneca 4.23: With Roman stoicism, the philosopher becomes the pedagogue of humankind. This expression is from Seneca: generis humani paedagogus. Seneca is prime minister. Marcus Aurelius is emperor.

*

From the beginning to the end of its history, philosophy was fascinated by the proximity of power (by the influence that it exerted over the mind of him whom it instructs). A philosopher is attracted by the organization of the State in which he lives like a butterfly lingering over and flying furiously around the burning flame. Why does a philosopher run after a tyrant? Why does Plato bustle around Dionysius I of Syracuse? Why does Aristotle follow Emperor Alexander? Why Seneca Emperor Nero? Why Descartes the Queen of Sweden? Why Diderot the Empress of Russia? Why Hegel Emperor Napoleon? Why Heidegger Chancellor Hitler? Not only does Plato rush to Dionysius I of Syracuse upon the very first request that he receives, but a single time does not suffice for his 'wisdom'. A second time, he climbs into the galley and exposes himself to death and to slavery, so much does the desire that his thought dominate the group haunt him. Seneca runs to Nero and, although facing rebuffs, humiliations and threats, asks for more until he ends up killing himself to obey the order that he has received from the emperor. Heidegger signs up as a member of the National Socialist Party, displays a total ingratitude to his Jewish mentors, raises his arm, wants to become the rector, becomes the rector. Why is philosophy socially so adhesive? Why can philosophy even become a subject for a national educational programme? Why did philosophers, who were the inheritors of the schools of Greece, become functionaries in order to culminate, for this highest value, at the top of the school system? Even at the first moment of this strange era, why does Socrates prefer a democratic death to the escape that his friends outline for him and have prepared for him? Whereas all Taoist, Buddhist, Indian,

Chinese, Korean and Japanese monks would have slipped away on the spot, would have made a point of honour out of escaping the will of the municipal house or the imperial house, of bolting away forthwith when facing their fellow creatures' hate, would have been delighted to have known how to flee from the claws and lances of warriors and from the ascendancy of the prince. Why is Descartes going to throw himself at Christine's feet to die of the cold? Why does Kant turn off his walk, at the coaching inn, to learn Robespierre's news? Why does Hegel fall into ecstasy in front of the invader riding by on a horse?

Even Schelling felt ashamed for Hegel.

*

The philosopher Victor Cousin opposed humanists to individuals, religious people to atheists, citizens to wanderers. In 1847, Victor Cousin wrote in *Cours de l'Histoire de la philosophie moderne* 1.179: 'Individuals claim to be the originals of the human species; they form a separate class; they make themselves out to be heroes of independence, and they are human beings without energy and without character; they fidget for a minute without doing anything, and pass through History without leaving a trace. In that they are undisciplinable, unworthy of being commanded and incapable of obeying, what is their great goal of representing on this immense stage of the world on which they spend a moment? Themselves, and nothing more. No one therefore pays attention to them; for humanity does not have enough time to waste on taking care of individuals who are but individuals.

*

Thought is secessive and the community excommunicates human beings who do not adhere to the custom of the place or who withdraw from the statistical law of the group or who distance themselves from the standardized usage of the national language spoken by everyone.

*

The origin of intellectual psychic activity is undertaken alone. Like phantasmagory which sets forth what is dreamt during the day, it is radically masturbatory. It is of an anti-parental as much as of an anti-reproductive nature. This is why intelligence becomes anti-familial. This is why thought is self-sufficient in an ever more antisocial manner. Its interrogation extends in an uncontrollable way, in an unappeasable mode. It tears itself away from oral society, from the prescriptive voice, from wisdom, from gods, from interdicts, from proverbs, from oracles.

*

Socrates dies at the heart of the group, surrounded by his friends. This is how he prefers to die: at the heart of the city in which he was born. But Socrates says to his friends, when he is in prison:

'The object of our desire is not truth but thought.'

Plato precisely writes in *Phaedo* 66e: We are lovers of thought. In Greek: We are the erastai of the phronesis. And he adds, in order to be even more precise: The thinker is the erastes of the place where *language makes a sign* (logos semainei). With this, Plato ceases to be a philosopher, leaves Dionysius the tyrant, becomes a thinker.

*

Writing is that strange process by which the continuous mass of language, once broken in silence, crumbles in the form of small unbound signs whose provenance is revealed to be extraordinarily contingent during the history that precedes birth. This alphabet is already a ruin. By means of this mutation, every 'sense' is decontextualized. Every signal becoming a sign loses its injunction, all the while losing its sound in the silence. Every sign is then decomposed and becomes littera that is dead, non-coercive, interpretable, transferable, transferential, transportable, ludic.

The noesis refers to the neotenic state of the brain, free of impressions, unaffected, larval, premature. Nativitas followed by lucidatio. A thought is always a newborn. The fact of thinking is always the brain elaborating itself—which comes out into the light while emitting an intractable cry.

A thinker is thus a human being who endows him- or herself with the most differentiated possible psychic activity. A human individuality that is the most alone possible. A hero that is the least mythic possible. The thinker is he or she who occupies the emptiest place possible.

*

Scholium.

Whoever writes has no place. He or she loses his or her place. Every *noesis* remains at the hunting stage. Whoever goes hunting loses his place ('you leave it, you lose it'). Whoever writes loses his place. Whoever thinks loses his place. He abandons his book in the temple of Diana the Huntress, plunges into the forest, climbs the mountain.

CHAPTER 34

Refugium

Serge Moscovici suddenly writes in his *Mémoirs* this sentence which abruptly rends the heart with its simplicity: 'One of the great strokes of luck that one can have in life is to have been unhappy in childhood.' This misfortune defuses for ever. At least in the time remaining for survival, it remains like an empty coffer. A rowboat that has never been occupied. Moscovici then evokes the Jewish Passover. A strange truce. Or, more exactly, a strange parenthesis in the social flux. An incredible annual epoche. A feast that fetes a flight. The most subversive dream that humanity has nurtured is this mysterious and pressing duty to which the soul beckons to emancipate itself from the preceding oppression.

It is always a matter of leaving Egypt forthwith.

It is a matter of dis-enslaving oneself.

An 'I'm leaving' works on the body which emerges into the atmospheric world.

A desire, which is not repressed and which dates back to birth, to have a run for it, until one becomes breathless.

However, if leaving slavery raises the question of fleeing, fleeing raises another question, a perhaps deeper one than that magnificent exeo. A question more ancient than that exit, than that ecstasy. The true question concealed in the fleeing of the slave—of the pursued prey—is that of refuge.

The true question raised by fleeing, behind that of refuge, concerns the ambivalence between claustrophilia and claustrophobia, both of which are originary, with one being prenatal, the other postnatal.

Birth already responds to the desire, in a state of panic, to go out.

If escaping raises numerous practical questions of short duration, living alone in a room raises questions of long duration, imposes a long apprenticeship, implies a metamorphosis followed by an ascesis of the preceding condition. This is the locus of conception.

*

This is why there is an old prayer—an anterior sup-
plication—at the heart of freedom. It hails a freedom from
the first world. It is this first-world freedom—this uterine,
solitary, Edenic quietude—which enables thought. At least
reading makes it necessary.

I will have belonged to those human beings for whom
study relayed this prayer. A first-world reclamation, that is,
without an object, that is, without content.

This empty, incredulous prayer prepares the dangerous
disinterestedness of thought.

Alexandre Koyré said that the exertion of thought
implied living in an impervious hideout which protected the
neophyte from the cruelty of human beings. Léo Strauss did
not think otherwise. Like Spinoza, before him.

Atheism—the empty container—is the nave of these
remains of a temple or church. One is never an atheist
except in a second period of time, after having freed oneself
from the memberships and fascinations of childhood. They
are ruins of a temple or a church: this empty afterbirth,
thrown into the garbage can at the hospital, tossed into
Sheol. This very poor memory of *beyond* haunts the
refugium.

The thinker's absorption inside his own thought—
beyond any state of alertness—is a prey's weakness offered
to violence.

This is how the true question for the pursued—even for the threatened—is that of refuge. Suddenly the living one must put his life in security. Giving refuge to life means 1. having affection for life, 2. increasing it (by increasing time).

However, thought presupposes the *loss* of the notion of time. If freedom of thought is having at one's unconditional disposal an *endless* time offered without any plan to its exertion, the worthwhile life is the refuge.

Living without being aware of it presupposes the refuge.

'Living without being on the alert' defines the refuge.

*

Pursued protestants wandered towards the 'refuge'. Such was the name given by shepherds, in the Alps, above Lake Geneva, to a little stone cabin that enabled the body to shield itself from the ferocity of wolves, from intense cold, from being seen by soldiers of any nation, and from the weight of the snow.

*

Thought is so far from conscience.

Oddly, thought is *conscienceless*.

Even as creative work, entirely absorbed in its object, defines par excellence conscienceless nervous activity.

There is nothing easier than killing a human being who is thinking, an animal which is sleeping.

A few intense instants of searching and stalking in the infinite and the unconscious presuppose a hideout, a roof, a pouch, a shelter: waiting in the garret until the pogrom passes by and its din turns at the corner and dies down. Gaining another day in one's hidden recess. O Lord, give me a day! Da nobis hodie!

*

Augustine wrote in his *Soliloquies*: There is in each human being a place (locus) where God can come and take shelter. This place to which God can come is a place built at the end of childhood, on the empty site of the lost container. It is the place re-hollowed out by language during its acquisition from the voice that cradled the hidden flesh and that has been lost. For it is that which invokes this voice that hails our Lord. This place is the mother who, by withdrawing, has transported it from her to the child, who has opened it inside himself by addressing him, and which thought thus re-joins.

*

At the end of Antiquity, Porphyry wrote in a more technical manner in his *Treatise of Abstinence*: Animals possess the *logos prophorikos* (the articulated voice), but they are not, for all that, *logikoi* (speakers) for lack of being invested with the *logos endiathetos* (language placed inside). If animals do not have this inner language (in a loop, which enables consciousness) which subjects human beings to what they hear, and which offers them up to social tyranny, they have the material sensation of the constitution of their bodies. Animals have a sensation of self-belonging.

The word *oikeiosis* used by Porphyry in this last sentence is extraordinary: for all the viviparous species, *the sentiment of belonging to a house* persists in the second world (where houses, nest, shells, pouches, shelters, lairs are indeed built). In this case, a house must be called a space of non-death.

✳

Thinking presupposes the conditions of sleeping but without sleeping.

Thinking presupposes otium, a cliff, security, the corner of two walls, a roof, the invisibility of the refuge, a constraint-free place, silence, recovered solitude and an empty, endless, alertless stretch of time.

The act of thinking presupposes 1. insouciance, 2. to be forgotten by the others. This is what partly defines the refuge. Not to matter in the eyes of others is priceless. Not to be important is a virtue. Forgetting one's fellow human beings also presupposes the exhilarating recompense of being forgotten by them. To be forgotten by the others becomes an ethical doctrine. This is what Zhuang Zhou called 'living invisibly at the end of the lane' (street, lane, way, called tao in Chinese).

*

The body must forget itself in order to think.

One must be alone to think and, moreover, be nothing and not be there. The house must be empty.

If it is also necessary that the 'run for your life' be absent from the body that manages to lose consciousness of itself, then, in the refuge, the insane idea of invulnerability progresses.

The mental dwelling presupposes familiarity, well-being, protection, elation, neither cold nor heat, neither hate nor love, shadow, floating ennui, aphonia. This world evokes a known world. The only fully known world was the initial water pouch in which the body was conceived and in which it developed. The refuge constitutes this known world which one knows like the back of one's hand, like one's 'pouch'.

*

To be free is thus to be in exile. Dependence goes back to the origin even as belonging is prenatal. Originarily, we are contained beings. One must find a modus vivendi between belonging and going astray. One must find a 'house' between nationalism and wandering.

A small corner.

At the heart of the *fuga* during which we expire while speaking, we die—this is the *refugium*.

Something takes shelter from the loss.

Living tranquilly and as little *oneself* and as *unknown* as in the first world.

CHAPTER 35

The Stove

Descartes' *poêle* (stove) is of the same derivation as the word *pensée* (thought), which it shelters. For the French word *poêle* derives from the Latin word 'pensilis', which *thinks* (*pense*) in that it derives from the *suspended* attic in which seeds and treasures can be kept away from predators. Thought depends on a warm refuge where the body does not recall itself to the soul: on a suspended haven, on a *pensoir*—a thinking place—in the air, on a nest in the branches, on a pensilis sublimis. In 1619, the sojourn in a warm room gives shelter, not only from winter but also from war. Thought needs a certain mouth of warmth, a cocoon of silence, a 'haber' of security on the seashore, a walled enclosure in the mountains, a yurt of sewn hides on the steppe, a tabernacle of impermeable canvas cloths in the desert.

But in Descartes' thought, that is, in the functioning of Descartes' thought, stove meant nothing other than his bed.

Descartes' attic, pensoir, poêle, pensilis formed a 'boat bed' for voyages.

One comes across Descartes' stove—which comes from the heart of the religious wars in the bloody Europe of the baroque world—in the 'blue boat' of aged Colette at the heart of the Second World War: totally insomniac, dying, she leans out the window, over Richelieu's garden (Palais-Royal), protecting her husband from being deported to the camps of Poland. Between Descartes and Colette, the couch that Freud offered to all his patients hesitates between the memories.

*

I am suddenly sure of it. I know. I no longer have a choice. I need to go up there to work. I need to separate myself from those who are down below. Impatient to be alone, I need to leap out of the world.

It is like the hourvari in the forest: the anxious roe deer suddenly bounds off his trail in order to be seen no longer, in order to be hounded no longer, in order to be tally-hoed no longer, in order not to die.

'Up there' is a little room under the roof. There is only a child's mattress, 80 centimetres in width, beneath a skylight. And there is only an old naked body which, every day, in the middle of the night, slips under the sheet, slips under the sky, slips under the moon, slips under the passing clouds, slips under the patter of the rain shower. If one day I don't go up there, if one day I don't take refuge from other human beings, the stints of malaise arise and the desire to die replaces the desire to flee. If I don't go up there even for an hour, on my bed of silence, seeing only the immense celestial depths by means of the dormer window which offers its light to the page, my ills dissolve, peace increases, the soul opens, I no longer suffer from anything, I forget myself, the inside of my mind not only sobers up but crumbles, my soul becomes transparent, translucid, if not lucid, if not soothsaying.

Centuries, families, children, nations dissolve up there.

A page of the sky ever legible between the tiles and the zinc window ledges.

Clouds of a thousand forms parade through this rectangle—this small templum which ornaments the ceiling with openwork and pierces the roof—project their shadows on the sheet of paper, on the wooden floor, on the whiteness of the bedsheet, even on the light fleece wool blanket.

This place, this handkerchief of a place, this sudariolum of a place, changing the bottle of water, changing the naked lightbulb which hangs at the end of its wire and admirably illumines the page being read or the page being written, washing the bedsheets, on the floor the little boxes containing the refills for the pens, tidying up, every Sunday, at the end of a work period, like a simple mass at a church, at least washing the floorboards with a sponge soaked in bleach for the pleasure of the little turned-up noses of the cats who carry out a meticulous inspection of it every twilight, working in this place, making my life necessary, more modest, more unshadowed, more offered, simpler.

My life becomes clearer as long as it becomes simpler, my thinner body becomes more absent, my emptier mind more eager.

*

There is a very strange experience which was brought to light by Descartes while reading in his 'pensilis' bed. It is not at all the fact of thinking (the cogitare), he says, which determines being. He asserts all of a sudden that thought must be perceived, even before all determination, as a *movement* which bears beings or silhouettes of beings or their names to inner consciousness.

Thought, he says, is a *thing* and this thing *moves*.

It is this *movement* which agitates the co-agitare of the breath that makes the soul (and not thematic thought), it is this movement which is born of birth, this terrible movement of the psychic intrusion of breath, which makes the ego sense its life and which makes it notice—even as white breath on lips in winter testifies to the movement of this breath which makes the soul, in an ever-unexpected way—its *constant* persistence during linguistic rumination. This is how—to retranslate into Greek these imprecise Latin concepts that Descartes employs while he is seeking to express this difficult sensation that he wants to put forward—an 'aion' resurfaces in the depths of the noetic chronos. There is an 'erstwhile exit' which each body renews while thinking, and which moves even in the apparent non-motivity of the body. This is the emotion of thinking. In all linguistic tenses, the whole social noetic chronicle is stirred by this lively scenting of prey, this more archaic temporal wave, at the limit of what is dreamt animally—*la rêvée animale*—which remains directly before the psychic breath. To this is added *constantly* the movement of being born. This reflection of thought *moving* in oneself like a thing in the body either forms a certain intimate pouch from scratch or finds the means to curl up again in a certain inner pouch that is already there.

In the depths of the thinker's psyche, prior to that which he thinks, there is something like the movement of a little one inside his mother.

This is why the turmoil of thought finds its total, theoretical, 'destinal' dimension in reading. For only in reading is the prenatal experience relayed.

It is not a 'me, I think' (ego cogito) which makes the heart of the soul. It is not a something evident, an identity, a truth. It is a movement, an emotion, a 'passio' specific to the 'res cogitans', itself experienced as essentially corporal, as independent in the soul.

It is the *movement* of thought (*motus* cogitationis).

This 'movement of thought' described by Descartes perhaps joins back up with that 'movement of flesh' (sarkos kinesis) that Sextus sought to indicate as our end (telos), arguing from the fact that it had been present at our beginning during the coition from which we originated.

Just as soon, beginning with this more internal movement (motus interior), the *ancient time* itself becomes the way of thinking (modus cogitandi) characteristic of human beings who think.

Not a content of thought (a noema) in the soul, not a position (the subject position) in the language, but an emotive recess, a kinesis in the opposite direction (nachträglich), a protection which envelops the anxious attentiveness and authorizes the following reflexion. To retranslate this into Latin, the res cogitans, before being a substantia,

is this motus exactly as the body is, during birth, this e-
motio (before being a body invaded by air, falling on the
ground into the light, it is this movement of issir). Time
precedes Being in this. The res cogitans, co-agitans, is not a
human head which looks but a surface which folds, which
folds back on itself, which hollows out its void inside a body
that sets off elsewhere. It is a minute cubicle relaying a
minute pouch inside an intracephalic cavern which extrava-
sates and suddenly rips open. It is a corner which enables
the acquired language to undergo an echoing phenomenon
which reverberates there, which resounds at the very instant
that it unfolds. It is this *recess* in which it rebounds. One of
Meister Eckhart's sermons is titled *On the Little Castle That
Is in the Soul* and recalls, if one muses about it, *The Empty
Fortress*, a beautiful book written by Bruno Bettelheim, who
took refuge in Chicago after he came back from the camp
of Buchenwald.

*

Epictetus said that thought is not a natural activity for the
body. He thought that the health of the soul was a dream—
and that noetic activity disturbed oneiric activity. Epictetus
wrote: 'Thought is a *passion* that *strikes* the soul *like a lightning bolt.*' The origin of thought is that there is a world *and*

then a second world. The origin of thought is that there is, inside the second world, a life as an infans *and then* a spoken language. The origin of thought is the incessantly present non-response to the incessantly unformulable question raised by the existence of natural languages among individual bodies. It is because human beings approached their milieu as non-responding that their enquiring began and that the origin surged forth as impassioned questioning, famished inquisitiveness, rhythmed by the seasons, interrupted by death.

*

To a certain degree of meditation, that is, of writing, that is, of reading, one no longer shares the earned view with anyone but oneself. One is alone in front of the invisible object about which one muses. Alone to discover the perspective, wholly new and even unheard-of to a certain extent, which leads there. Alone to be understood inside the new light that presses down on all the re-born in a new relief. At this degree of study and thought, solitude is much more than a sensitive fact; it is a mode of experience. One no longer has an interlocutor in immediate reality. No inventoriable reader in the group at this given moment. Inter-diction no longer occurs. An oeuvre alone therefore enables one to speak to oneself. A book enables one as a single person—and not as an ego—to communicate with the alter ego of each ego. Ego and alter ego are simple reflections of the reflexion which is invented inside the volume of the book and which is constructed part after part, articulation after articulation, organ after organ, mind after mind, chapter after chapter—in the same way that they are both pure grammatical persons of the language which grows silent and meditates there. The written oeuvre is God himself in a certain sense—for what God is in the oral dialogue, what is written is to thought. The written is not an Erstwhile God (preceded by eternity). The book is not an Eternal (judged by the law). It is the Alter that surges forth when the pages are half-opened. In *Ethica*, Spinoza, in Voorburg, communicated a little with himself. Then he hid the manuscript from anyone else's gaze, in a little wardrobe, even as the Romans, in the past, would hide their images, which were the skulls of their fathers. The oeuvre is the unfindable interlocution of thought. Writing thinks. To a certain degree of thought, one can no longer distinguish these verbs but only their order. Thinking cannot be written. Writing thinks. Writing finds that which he or she who has written could not think of without the written oeuvre.

CHAPTER 36

Locronan

When Locronan died, the Breton chieftains gathered together in the hermit's cave at the top of the hill. The saint's body had become entirely black. He was like granite over which water flows. And this granite block lay turned-over on the earth. Saint Ronan came to see Locronan dead. Redbad also came to say goodbye. Alke also said goodbye. Aditi came. The Twelve surrounded him in silence.

Then one of the chieftains began to speak. He said:

'During his lifetime, we were never able to understand him. It was easier to draw the flight of a swallow in the sky than to follow the tracks of the thought of this solitary, foul-mouthed man. Therefore, now that he is dead, here is what I propose: May he do as he pleases! We're going to yoke the oxen. They'll drag this corpse. They'll know how to lead us to where he wants to be buried!

They then untied the oxen. The bulls and the oxen had a hard time dragging that piece of granite. During this time, the chieftains, examining the tracks left by the stone in the rumpled branches of the heath, the crushed black and yellow leaves, the incised, excavated mud, tried to understand what the saint had said.

Aeschylus wrote in verse 93 of *The Suppliants*: The ways of thought head towards their goal through thickets and dense shadows.

The tracks left by the stone led the chieftains into the darkness of the forest. However, the oxen and the saint's body crossed the forest. Afterwards, they arrived in a prairie. There, the oxen suddenly came to a halt. They trampled the daffodils. The daffodils were torn out by handfuls and the ground was opened. The men dug at exactly the spot where the oxen had stopped. The air was brisk. A ray of sunlight separated the youngest leaves that had grown in the blue air; the icy wind touched the little yellow bells and made them bend, sway, tremble, dance. The body was brought down with ropes. The body was too heavy. Then, at a given moment, the body fell. It was cold, but the sunlight was beautiful. The grouses crowed. The cuckoos warbled. A little chapel was built above the grave in which they had lain the stone and that they had covered over with the dirt that they had removed while digging.

With a few exceptions (for reasons of clarity in English), I have systematically followed Quignard's particular use of italics and quotation marks (or the lack thereof) for foreign terms, foreign phrases, and various key words.

PAGE 1 | **Redbad:** Quignard writes 'Rachord', the French spelling of the Frisian king's name such as it appears in French translations of Jacobus de Varagine's *Golden Legend*, originally written in Latin (1261–66). The king's Latin name is Rachordus. Variants in contemporary French research and translations are Redbad, Radbod or Ratbod. In English, the king's name is usually spelled Redbad or Radbod. In his text, Quignard uses both Rachord and Rachodus. The king lived between *c.*679–719.

PAGE 3 | **Originary,** which translates the French word *originaire*, is a key word in this book. Now considered obsolete or archaic in English, it means native, originating, primal.

PAGE 17 | **sense of smell:** Here, and subsequently throughout the book, Quignard develops the key concept of the *flair*, whose English meanings and connotations differ from the French term. The French *flair* indicates the sense of smell, scenting, intuition, even the 'sixth sense'. Quignard will likewise underscore the importance of 'sniffing' (*reniflement*), as an element in this *flair*.

PAGE 24 | **what is dreamt**: A translation of Quignard's phrase *la rêvée*, elsewhere translated in the work as 'the dreamt'. In other words, the content of a dream.

PAGE 26 | *connaître*—**to be acquainted**: When Quignard dissects the French verb *connaître*, which (like *savoir*) is often translated into English as 'to know', I juxtapose it to and translate it by the English verb 'to be acquainted with'. The etymology of 'acquaint' goes back, through Old French, to Vulgar Latin *accognitare* (to make known), from Latin *accognitus* (acquainted with), which is the past participle of *accognoscere* (to know well), from the preposition *ad* and *cognitus*, the past participle of *cognoscere* (to come to know). Similarly, the etymology of the French verb *connaître* also goes back to *cognoscere*. This meaning of 'to be acquainted with' enables me to differentiate the two French verbs *savoir* and *connaître*.

PAGE 34 | **the magnetization of the beloved towards the magnet, the lover**: The French word *aimant* means 'magnet' as well as, literally, 'one who loves', the 'lover'. Two distinct etymologies are involved, but the spelling is the same, enabling Quignard to make this pun.

PAGE 34 | **the erstwhile:** I have adopted Chris Turner's solution for Quignard's key word and concept 'le Jadis', as explained in his translator's note to *The Sexual Night* ([London: Seagull Books, 2014], p. 158) and in Quignard's text itself in that book: 'In Old French, *jadis* breaks down into a *ja y a dies*—already there was a day. In Modern English, we should unpack this almost incomprehensible sequence—Already, in the past, there was there is.'

PAGE 52 | **the great heartrending, amplifying, native void, itself lost inside the loss, leaving the Lost in space:** The French phrase for 'the Lost' is *la Perdue*, in the feminine case. Arguably, given the context, this *Perdue* could be interpreted as 'the Lost Mother', or perhaps 'the Lost Origin', but the author leaves this issue open. In other instances, he writes *le perdu*, in the masculine case, referring more generally to that which has been lost.

PAGE 72 | **The mother uses the *Tu* infinitely:** The *tu* evoked by Quignard is the familiar form of address, as opposed to the *vous*.

PAGE 76 | **across from Gnosis:** In the French, Quignard uses the spelling *Gnose*, recalling *Gnosis*, for Knossos. At the end of the same chapter, Liber is a Roman god associated with viticulture, wine, fertility and freedom, in other words a Romanized version of Dionysus, Ariadne's husband. The name *Liber* comes from a proto-Italic term meaning 'belonging to the people' and therefore 'free'. One notes that *liber* means 'book' in Latin.

PAGE 89 | **If the hero already possesses a *nom* (name), then he is 'renamed' and obtains *renom* (renown)**: The English word 'renown' derives from Anglo-French *renoun*, from Old French *renon* 'renown, fame, reputation,' from *renomer* 'make famous,' from *re-* + *nomer* ('to name'), from Latin *nominare* 'to name'. Hence, similarly, 'renown' is to have been 'renamed'.

PAGE 92 | **Pasts that pass back over their past passages**: In French: *Passés qui repassent dans leurs passées.* Quignard puns with *passé* (past) and *passée* (a hunting term meaning the trail or passage habitually used by the wild game that one is hunting).

PAGE 104 | **the ev-angile (go-spel)**: The etymology of the English word 'gospel' mirrors the French word *evangile* and the archaic English word 'evangel'. Old English *gōdspel*, from *gōd* 'good' + *spel* 'news, a story', translating ecclesiastical Latin *bona annuntiatio* or *bonus nuntius*, used to gloss ecclesiastical Latin *evangelium*, from Greek *euangelion* 'good news'; after the vowel was shortened in Old English, the first syllable was mistaken for *god* 'God'. The archaic English word 'evangel' is from Middle English (in the sense 'gospel'): from Old French *evangile*, via ecclesiastical Latin from Greek *euangelion* 'good news', from *euangelos* 'bringing good news', from *eu-* 'well' + *angelein* 'announce'.

PAGE 109 | **A silence—an *en-fance* (infans, childhood)—is thus led to war by language:** Quignard alludes to the etymology of the French word *enfance*, from Latin *infans*, from the privative prefix *in-* and *fans*, the present participle of *for*, *fari* ('to speak'). It follows that an 'infant' is 'one who cannot yet speak'.

PAGE 119 | **There is no Ancient Greek word for 'consciousness':** The French word for 'conscience' is *conscience*, but in English we also have 'conscious' and 'consciousness'. Depending on the context, I have opted for 'conscience' or 'consciousness' as the translation of *conscience*, but the reader should keep in mind that our English semantic distinctions between 'conscious' and 'conscient', between 'consciousness' and 'conscience', sometimes overlap in the single French term.

PAGE 136 | **the first lines of the invocation to Venus which opens Lucretius' *De natura rerum*:** Lucretius, *On the Nature of Things* (Cyril Bailey trans.) (Oxford: Clarendon Press, 1948[1910]).

PAGE 176 | In his evocation of conversations with **Alain Didier-Weil,** Quignard puns with the common French expression *donner sa langue au chat*, which means that 'one gives up and awaits an answer'. Here, Quignard writes *on leur donnait la langue*, by which he means literally that the two men 'gave the tongue, the language, to the cats' and therefore that the cats could now speak and answer Didier-Weil's question.

PAGE 187 | **a tact that has its own contact**: Quignard introduces *tact* in its etymological sense, from the Latin word *tactus* 'a touch, handling, sense of touch', from the verb *tangere* 'to touch'.

PAGE 188 | **coire-coïtare**: Quignard plays with the various senses of the Latin verb *coire* means 'to copulate', 'to encounter', 'to come up against', 'to assemble', 'to meet', 'to come together', 'to unite', 'to ball up', etc. *Coïtare* is an obsolete French verb meaning 'to cogitate', 'to think'.

PAGE 189 | **Issir**: From the Old French *issir, eissir*, from Latin *exeo, exire*, 'to exit', 'to leave', 'to go out'.

PAGE 192 | **A kind of Erstwhile from which the beast *rushes***: Quignard uses the verb *foncer*, which means 'to rush', 'to charge', 'to make a straight line to', but he is implicitly underscoring its etymology: from *fons*, an ancient form of *fond, fonds* (bottom, base, foundation). The next sentence, about Archimedes, also uses the verb *foncer*.

PAGE 204 | ***Bêtise*—stupidity . . . the forte of animals**: Underscoring the animal origins of humankind, Quignard puns with *bête* (beast, animal) and *bêtise* (stupidity), and continues punning throughout the paragraph. My paraphrase recalls Psalm 73:22, in the Good News Translation: 'I was as stupid as an animal. I did not understand you.' King James Version: 'So foolish was I, and ignorant; I was as a beast before thee.' In English, a cognate like 'beastliness' has a different meaning.

<small>PAGE</small> **231 | like one's 'pouch':** *comme sa poche.* This is an untranslatable pun with the two meanings of *poche*: 'pouch' and 'pocket'.